DELTA
ADRIFT

THE GOLDEN OCELOT, BOOK 2

DELTA
ADRIFT

JESSE HAYNES

This is a work of fiction. Names, characters, places, and incidents either are the product of the author's imagination or are used fictitiously. Any resemblance to actual persons, living or dead, events, or locales is entirely coincidental.

Copyright © 2021 by Jesse Haynes

All rights reserved. No part of this book may be reproduced or used in any manner without written permission of the copyright owner except for the use of quotations in a book review. For more information, address: castlebuilderspress@gmail.com.

First paperback edition October 2021.

Book design by Allen Jenkins

ISBN: 978-1-7344723-3-2

www.castlebuilderspress.com

*To Grant Eastman.
A great friend who edited
a number of 5 outta 10 manuscrupts
while I napped.*

ONE:
PARIS AIR

"Be back here at a quarter to midnight. Same place."

"Yes sir. Enjoy your night."

"Yeah."

Money changed hands, then a man in a black suit climbed out of the back seat of a dark limousine. He adjusted his tie then nodded at his reflection in the tinted window as the limousine drove away.

The man scanned the people on the street, careful not to make any eye contact, then turned to the mansion behind him. Even from the street, he could hear the live jazz music drifting his way from inside, floating through the Paris air like the evening breeze.

As he looked at the mansion, apprehension knotted in the man's stomach. This didn't feel like it used to. He was slowing down—trying to get out of the game, even. After a long exhalation, he walked through the front gates and down the cobblestone sidewalk, his shoes clicking as he walked.

The mansion's white exterior was illuminated to highlight the swooping arches and balconies. A fountain outside the breezeway spilled water into a burbling stream that ran along the sidewalk. He walked alongside it, heading upstream.

When he reached the front doors of the mansion, he was greeted by a doorman in a red jacket and matching tie. "May I ask your name?"

"Klaw."

"Do you have a last name, Mr. Klaw?" The doorman was overly friendly, the type of person who could put a price tag on a smile.

"Nope. Just Klaw. With a K."

"Alrighty then." Skeptically, the greeter scrolled through a list of names on his tablet before arching an eyebrow. "Wow, um, here you are, Klaw."

"Good deal."

"Okay, enjoy the party, uh... *Klaw*."

"Yeah."

The greeter pulled one of the doors open and Klaw slipped inside.

Immediately, the music swelled as it pulled him through the entryway and welcomed him into a ballroom full of at least three hundred people. Inside, all the men wore fancy suits and the women were adorned in designer dresses and jewels.

Some people were talking, wine glasses in hand, while others drunkenly swayed arm-in-arm to a live band that performed from a stage against the south wall, which was actually more of a giant panel of windows. A table of hors d'oeuvres was spread out on the opposite wall, while waiters carried trays of more food and drinks to the people who milled about.

The ballroom smelled of money. Or at least it did to Klaw. Not the actual smell of paper bills, but the smell of wealth. The smell of what money will buy if you're rich enough, powerful enough, or reckless enough to want it: High-end perfumes mixed with expensive alcohols. Cologne and fine foods. The overpowering fragrance of wealth and extravagance.

But Klaw wasn't there for the party. There was something much more important he needed to attend to.

This was business.

He began moving through the ballroom, pressing through the crowd slowly but purposefully.

"Monsieur, can I interest you in a glass of wine?" a young man carrying a tray of wine glasses asked him.

"Don't think I've ever said no to that question." Klaw took a glass from the waiter.

"It's 2005. A local vintage, too. You're in for a treat."

Klaw took a sip. "Yeah, tastes... local."

Navigating a room full of music, people, and dancing was no easy task. He took out his phone and reread the notes he'd written the previous night: *Up stairwell at end of the ballroom. Down a hallway. Last door on the right.* Those were the instructions.

He spotted the stairwell on the other side of the room, mumbling his distaste as he continued to traverse the crowd. A woman to his left reached out and grabbed his coat. He turned to her and was met with a glazed-over gaze.

She'd had too much to drink. *Way* too much.

Reluctantly, he asked, "Um, can I help you?"

"Yeah. Do I know you?" she slurred. "You look familiar." The woman was mid-thirties. Very attractive. Even more intoxicated.

"I don't think we've met," Klaw answered back. "And now's not the best time. I need to be going."

"No, you don't! The night is still young." The woman stepped forward, giggling, and put her hand on the breast pocket of Klaw's blazer. "Did you come here with anyone?" She reeked of the wealth-smell, but this time it was up close.

"No, but—" Klaw instantly regretted his answer before he'd finished it.

"Then give me a dance! I promise you, you will enjoy it." She gave her best attempt at a flirtatious wink, but it came across more like an eye convulsion.

"I think you better sit down, ma'am."

"Nonsense!" she objected. "This is a really big house. How about we go find our own room and… dance?"

"I'm—" Klaw began.

"…Tall. Dark. Handsome." She cut him off, taking two fingers and walking them up his chest to his shoulder.

"Listen." He was beginning to lose his patience. "I don't have time for this. I'm not here for the party. I'm here on business."

"Oh… security?"

Klaw let out a sigh and tapped a second woman who was standing beside him. "Hey, miss?"

She turned toward him. "Hello?"

"Hey… can you do me a favor?"

"Sure."

Klaw pushed the first woman toward the second. "I need to run to the restroom, but my friend here really needs somebody to watch her. Would you mind?"

The second woman immediately took in the drunkenness of the first. "It's no problem at all," she said as she took the woman by the hand. "Here, hon, let's go get you some canapes."

"Thanks a lot."

Klaw left. He wasn't coming back.

He fought through the room of people with more haste, pulling up the sleeve of his jacket and checking his watch. His pace quickened even more. When he finally reached the stairs, he took them two at a time.

Behind him, the party roared on.

Klaw reached the top of the stairs, found the hallway, and headed down it. At the end, he double-checked the instructions on his phone one last time. This was it. He'd found it. He drained his wine glass as anticipation stirred within him.

He knocked on the door, which swung open almost instantly. A large, burly man stood on the other side, a pistol holstered to his belt. He made eye contact with Klaw, nodded in recognition, and then stepped back.

This room was just as lavish as the ballroom, only smaller. It was an office with off-white walls, decorative plants, vases, and a desk across the room. Behind the desk was a painting—some expensive original work of a dead Frenchman, no doubt.

And more importantly, on the far side of the desk sat a man: mid-fifties, graying hair, expensive suit, round spectacles, thin smile.

The man met Klaw's eyes and said, "Such a pleasure to finally meet you in person." He stood, walking around the desk to greet his guest.

"Mr. Gobert, I echo your sentiment." Klaw shook the hand that was offered.

Gobert looked toward the burly security man. "Theo, you may be excused. Get yourself something to drink."

"Yes sir. Thank you." Theo left the room, pulling the door shut behind him.

Once they were alone, Gobert wasted no time at all. "Let's talk business," he said. "Please, have a seat."

Klaw obliged, sitting down in a chair opposite the desk. Gobert also sat, taking out a bottle of wine. "Would you like a drink?"

Klaw still had his empty wine glass in one hand. "I'm really liking your house," he quipped as he handed the glass over to Gobert, but the man took a clean one from under his desk and filled it before handing it over.

"Chateau Lafite, 1865," Gobert explained. "I've been saving it for a special occasion such as this."

Klaw took the wineglass and peered into the crimson liquid before swirling it around. He was holding a bit of history. "1865, you say?"

"*Oui*, from here in France," Gobert confirmed. "I believe this runs about twenty-five thousand American dollars per bottle."

The wine glass suddenly seemed heavier in Klaw's hand. He arched an eyebrow. "You don't say? I appreciate the generosity."

"This is a big occasion. It's not every day that such events can be celebrated." Gobert poured himself a glass.

"I see." Klaw took a drink of the savory wine, tasting it thoughtfully and wondering why this one demanded a higher price than any of his favorite grocery-store selections. "What events are you referring to, exactly?"

Gobert took a sip then asked, "Do you know why I invited you here?"

Klaw shrugged. "I'm sure there's more to it than simply sharing a drink."

Gobert nodded, then asked a question that seemed unrelated. "How much do you know of my work, Klaw?"

Almost mechanically, Klaw recited, "You're a software superpower and your company, Spark, is aggressively absorbing the competition via acquisitions. I know you service nearly half of America's Fortune 500 companies for business analytic programs with your Spark Company."

"Yes, fantastic." Gobert took another sip and smiled. "What a marvelous drink. Don't you agree?"

"Oh yes."

Gobert set down his glass. "Do you know how Spark ranks in sales for all SaaS companies?"

"Sass?"

"Software as a service."

"Oh." Klaw nodded. "Top two."

"*Exactly*." Gobert laid a manilla folder on his desk, opening it to a spreadsheet. "In 2006, when I founded Spark, we were outside the top 50 in terms of sales volume. Three years ago, we were number four. This year, after Steamroller, Spark has become a multibillion-dollar business. This is a red ocean we're swimming in, but we're still thriving, my friend."

Slightly confused, Klaw took a sip of wine. "Sounds like you're moving in the right direction."

Gobert nodded. "We are. We've climbed and climbed, but now there's nowhere else to climb. Spark has gone as high as the industry's ceiling will allow… for now."

Klaw let out a huff of sudden understanding. "And that's the job, isn't it?"

"Exactly." Gobert leaned back in his seat. "The higher you climb the ladder, the harder it is to keep going. You understand that, right?"

"I do."

"So do you know what that means?"

Klaw looked back down to his wine and smirked. "You want me to provide a catalyst? Something to help you climb to the top?"

"Precisely."

"Do you have anything particular in mind?

Gobert took another paper out of the folder. It was a logo: a red "E" with two blue stripes down the side. "I want to make a play on the direct competition."

Klaw recognized it immediately. "Edge," he said. "The number one software company in the world."

Gobert scowled. "We are making better programs, but Edge has been in the industry for a long time and has much more brand recognition and customer loyalty. That alone is enough to consistently draw large partners to their products. People know their work and trust them, so they get the business."

"Basically, the same reason you scheduled to meet with me," Klaw pointed out. "I've been doing this for a long time."

"Exactly. But I need Edge to stumble, and the only way I can see this happening is if something happens to their leadership."

Klaw finished his wine. "Just tell me what you want me to do."

For the first time, Gobert looked uncomfortable,

like he had come this far but still was struggling to actually say the words.

"It's fine," Klaw offered. "I've heard... *everything.*"

Gobert opened his mouth, froze, then tried again. On his second effort, he formed the words. "I want to hire you to eliminate the CEO of Edge, and it *must* look like an accident. The loss of their founder and mastermind is enough for Spark to overtake them."

The faintest grin stretched across Klaw's face. This wasn't going to be an easy job, but it would certainly be worthwhile. "I figured you must have had something big planned for the price you mentioned on the phone."

"Fifty-million U.S. dollars," Gobert reiterated.

"I know what you said. But you're asking me to kill a tech giant. That's not going to be easy."

"You want more?"

"Make it one-hundred million dollars."

"Seventy."

"Seventy-five."

"Done." The two men shook hands, as Gobert added, "And, as you know, in no way will I be linked to the hit."

"Goes without saying." Klaw nearly laughed. "Just give me the man's name and two weeks to get the job done."

Gobert took a picture from the folder and set it before Klaw. It showed a smiling, bespectacled man with salt-and-pepper hair. "Brimley is his name. Stuart Brimley."

Klaw nodded. "I see. Starting tonight, Mr. Stuart Brimley has two weeks to live."

TWO:
GOOD DAY USA

The beautiful woman walking onto the stage was completely unphased by the blinding lights and the deafening applause.

She entered from the left of the stage and announced to the studio crowd, "Good morning, and thank you for tuning into another episode of Good Day, U.S.A! It's Friday, the twenty-second of July, and we have an impressive line-up for this morning's show, let me tell you!"

More raucous applause came until the signs fixed above the stage quieted everybody by flashing a short message: *Silent!*

The woman, still smiling, sat down on a leather armchair in the middle of the set. A backdrop behind her was decorated with a few potted plants and a sign that read *GOOD DAY, U.S.A.*

As the applause died down, she added, "As always, I'm your host, Emilia Pepperside."

"I love you, Emilia!" someone yelled from the studio

audience.

Despite the aggressive flashing of the *Silent!* signs once again, she held a hand to her heart before continuing. "I hope all of you are having a fantastic morning. Let's try to get your day started right!"

The signs' message changed to *Applause!* As prompted, the audience clapped.

Emilia waited for the cheers to quiet down, then said, "As you all know, I am a huge supporter of charities. They are phenomenal, and I was extremely honored when *People Magazine* recently wrote that through my constant involvement with charities, I am trying to save the world."

More applause.

She went on. "That is the ultimate compliment in my eyes, but you see, I am only *trying* to save the world. Today, it's my pleasure to introduce somebody who has *actually* saved it. Ladies and gentlemen, please put your hands together for the teenage hero, Shafer McCartney!"

Hearing his name made Shafer's breathing quicken. From where he stood backstage, he could see only part of the large studio audience, but that was more than enough to make him uneasy. And while this wasn't his first TV appearance over the last two weeks—far from it, even—the nerves still got the best of him.

He didn't have much time to worry, though, because he was nudged gently from behind by one of the producers, a forty-something-year-old man with a bulky headset and clipboard. "All right, kid. You're on. Good luck."

With a deep breath, Shafer walked onto the set from behind the backdrop. He tried to force a smile, but he was sure it looked more like a pained grimace as the stage lights hit him square in the face. He raised his hand to block out the light—a gesture that was mistaken as a wave.

The audience went crazy. People stood, clapping and cheering loudly enough that the stage trembled from the sheer volume. On the front row, Shafer spotted two younger females. Both were wearing a shirt adorned with his face.

This had become Shafer's life. He was a national sensation, and after being discharged from the hospital a month ago he had been whisked across the country, appearing on talk shows, doing radio and podcast interviews, talking to reporters, and providing everything else the media had demanded from him.

America could not get enough of Shafer McCartney, and there was no refusing the demands of the press—or *escaping* the press, for that matter.

It had been exhausting, too. He'd been living on lots of coffee and very little sleep, trying to stay in contact with the people close to him but rarely even having time to pick up his phone.

He smiled as Emilia stood and shook his hand, offering him a spot on the leather armchair beside hers. They both sat.

When the applause finally died down once again, she said, "Shafer, it's *fantastic* to have you on this morning's show. Thank you so much for joining us."

"It's no problem, really," he responded, trying to sound as relaxed as possible, just as he'd been taught. "Thanks for having me, by the way."

"It's our pleasure," Emilia answered with a warm nod. "You were by far the most requested guest by our viewers. And, speaking of those viewers, I have a big question for you. I think I already know the answer, but I have to ask anyway."

With everything that had been asked of him in the last two weeks, Shafer had no doubts that he could handle anything thrown his way. "Sure, fire away."

With twinkling eyes, she leaned in close and loudly whispered, "Shafer McCartney, are you single?"

Laughter came from all around the studio.

Shafer arched an eyebrow. "Are you asking for *personal* reasons, Ms. Pepperside?" he replied with a joking grin. "I'm seventeen."

She waved her hand with a playful dismissiveness. "No, I'm asking for all the teenage girls across the country who are so obsessed with you."

"Okay, good deal. You don't seem like a cougar—can I say that on air?"

"I don't see why not." Emilia crossed one leg over the other, leaned back in her seat, and then said, "I have so much that I'd like to ask you that I just don't know where to begin."

"That's fine. I mean, if you want, we could always just sit here and chill for half an hour. I could use the rest. I'm not sure how me napping on-air would impact your ratings, but I'm totally down to find out."

Emilia chuckled. "Then I guess I better start asking questions because your time is way too valuable for me to miss out on this chance to talk."

"Oh, you're too kind."

She looked towards the audience. "By this time, all of you know the story of Shafer McCartney: the teenage savior who killed a dangerous domestic terrorist, free-fell from a plane, foiled a plot to detonate a nuclear bomb in the nation's capital, and then defeated a small army of robots who intended to enslave humanity. Shafer is a national hero."

As he listened, Shafer didn't know what to do. Nodding his head would make him seem arrogant. Doing nothing would make him seem boring. He ultimately opted to just smile, although his cheeks were already tired. *How did people smile so much?*

Emilia turned to him. "So tell me, Shafer, when did you realize just how big you've become? Did you have an 'oh-snap, I'm an A-list celebrity' moment?"

He contemplated this. Despite his number of recent interviews, this question was new. How big *had* he become?

Finally, he managed, "Um, I think A-list is pushing it. But I did have that kind of experience when I saw somebody wearing a *Shafer McCartney for President* t-shirt."

Emilia laughed, a bubbly sound that no doubt had taken lots of practice.

Before she could ask anything else, he added, "And I would like to point out that in no way am I affiliated with that, nor do I know where they are coming from."

"It's funny because I too have seen those shirts," Emilia said. "But I can assume you're not putting your name in the hat for the upcoming presidential election?"

"Not until I get older," he joked.

"You do have some political ties in your family, though."

"You mean my uncle?"

"Yes. Would you like to share?"

"Sure. He's the director of the FBI."

"And you live with him and your aunt?"

Shafer nodded. "I do. They're like parents to me. They've raised me. My parents were FBI too, but they died in a fire when I was really little, and..." He trailed off, suddenly realizing he was probably oversharing for a happy-go-lucky morning show. "You know, we don't need to go there."

Emilia didn't miss a beat. "Growing up around the FBI had to make an impact on you. Is that what inspired your knack for adventure and heroics?"

Shafer rubbed his chin, thinking. "I mean, yes and no. I always wanted to be an agent when I was little because it's always been a family thing, but at the end of the day, I'm just the kind of person that loves adventure. That wouldn't be any different if my uncle was a baker or an accountant."

"I see. So, what's your next chapter with the FBI? Any more missions in the foreseeable future?"

Emilia could somehow speak to both Shafer *and* the studio audience at the same time.

Shafer wasn't sure if she was serious or not, but he adamantly shook his head. "That's a hard no. I quickly realized that one mission was enough for me, and I'm very content being a high school student, then going to college. We'll figure out what's next later."

"High school will be interesting, I'm sure," Emilia said. "You're starting your senior year soon, but now you're such a revered celebrity. Any plans of homeschooling?"

"No, I'm going back to my school when summer's over. I'm trying to keep my life as normal as possible."

"So, you'll be the American idol trying to get to biology class in time?"

Shafer calmly shook his head. "I'm just a normal teenager, I swear. I haven't done anything intended to be *heroic*, just the things I knew I needed to do. I wasn't trying to become famous or whatever, I promise. That's not my style."

"It's interesting to hear you say that," she answered, "because that leads into my next question. Do you consider yourself to be extremely lucky, or extremely unlucky?"

"Geez, I don't know who comes up with these questions, but that's another hard one," Shafer smirked. "I guess I'm a combo of both. I'm super unlucky because I got into so many situations where I knew that I was a goner, but I also somehow survived, so I guess I'm lucky as well."

"From what I've heard, you certainly stared death in the face countless times. Like you just hinted at, you were in a lot of tight spots. If you're comfortable talking about it, will you share if there were any certain points that you were positive you were going to be killed?"

This was the one question Shafer knew was coming, but only because he'd been asked for approval before the show. "Yeah, I knew I was dead right after I was sucked out of the airplane and started to freefall back to earth without a parachute. I didn't exactly like my odds at the time."

"I can imagine."

"At the end of the day, I'm just glad to be alive, and to be safe, and to be here." He gestured toward the audience, and there was a rumble of positive chatter until the audio team silenced them with the signs.

"And we're happy to have you. What's next for you,

Shafer?"

"I'm hoping for some lunch," he replied immediately.

Emilia let out that perfect laugh again, prompting, "I mean, I heard about some sort of ceremony tomorrow…"

He nodded. "Yeah, President Grady is holding a little reception tomorrow to give me an award. I said it was too much, but—"

Emilia jumped in, elaborating, "Tomorrow, Shafer's being honored with the new Shafer McCartney Award, which is for acts of bravery performed by a minor. That's got to feel pretty special, right Shafer?"

"Definitely. President Grady had been too good to me throughout the entire recovery."

Emilia asked, "So after your award, do you have anything else going on, Shafer?"

"Thankfully, that's it. Other than a little vacation." He smiled just thinking about it. The difference was that this smile, unlike most of his smiles from throughout the morning, wasn't forced.

"A vacation sounds much-needed after the month you've had."

"For sure. But apart from that, I'd be just as happy if my life went back to being normal. I want to go to school, play sports—all the normal stuff, y'know? Some Madden, too."

"Completely understandable, Shafer. And before we start winding down this segment, I've got to ask this: you don't seem like you necessarily like the extra attention, so apart from saving the world, did any good come out of your… experience?"

"Oh, for sure," Shafer grinned. "I made some great friends while I was there."

Emilia gave a knowing look before asking, "Do you mean friends like May Brimley?"

The name made Shafer's heartbeat quicken. "Yes, I was so lucky to meet her."

"I'm about to get nosey, but is she the official reason you aren't single?"

He nodded.

Emilia held up a finger. "Do you hear that?"

Confused, he asked, "What?"

"I thought I heard something..."

"Um, what did you hear?"

With twinkling eyes, Emilia said, "I just heard the sound of ten-thousand teenage hearts breaking."

Shafer laughed. "Oh, I don't know about that. I'm lucky that May is even putting up with me. I've been so busy I haven't even seen her really since I left the hospital. It's been nonstop, so I can't wait to see her again."

"Aww," Emilia cooed, turning towards the audience. "In case you don't know, May Brimley is Shafer's girlfriend, and she is the daughter of the computer software engineer, Stuart Brimley, who created the multi-award-winning computer program, Razor, along with dozens of other software programs."

There were nods from across the crowd. Everybody knew Stuart Brimley, and May's name had been getting a lot of attention lately too thanks to her association with Shafer.

Emilia playfully added, "May is also probably the most loathed girl in America. But, to be fair, she's got it all: she's both beautiful *and* intelligent. Don't you agree,

Shafer?"

May. Just the thought of her pulled him out of the studio. He missed everything about her: her smile, her eyes, the way she laughed at his bad jokes, and the way she could make him feel like he was the only person in the world. If only he could...

"Shafer, don't you agree?"

Emilia's question pulled him out of his deep thoughts. "What? Oh, um, yes. Definitely. She's amazing."

"Do you have any plans with her soon?"

"Actually, yes. That's the vacation I mentioned. The Brimley's were kind enough to invite me on a trip with them."

"Oh, that'll be fun! Any hints as to where you're going?"

Shafer shook his head. "My lips are sealed. I'm looking forward to laying low for a while, so I gotta make sure *nobody* knows where I'm at."

Emilia offered a smile that, in many ways, told Shafer she could personally relate. "I think that's excellent."

"I appreciate it."

She changed topics once more, saying, "All right, I've got one more question for you before we go to break."

"Go on..."

"Okay, Shafer, I've heard whisperings about a code name you used during your FBI mission: 'The Golden Ocelot?'"

Hearing the words made Shafer smirk. "I'm not sure where you got these whisperings, but yeah, that's me."

"Can you explain to me and our viewers the meaning behind it?"

Shafer explained, "Yeah, for sure. It's not too great

of a story, really, but I told my uncle that I wanted a cool codename for my FBI mission, and he told me that it was overkill. 'You don't need a codename for one mission, Shafe.' Something like that." Shafer gave the quote with his best Richard McCartney impression, triggering laughter throughout the studio

"But you insisted?" Emilia teased.

"Oh, for sure. If I was in the field, I *needed* a cool name."

"So why did you pick the Golden Ocelot?"

"Honestly? It was May's idea. Ocelots are small cats, and sometimes wildlife discounts how dangerous they can be. It seemed appropriate, especially with everything I'd been through at that point."

"That's a great story, Shafer," Emilia said. "And in all honesty, I had to Google 'ocelot' to even know what one looked like."

"Hey, same!"

They shared another laugh, and then Emilia glanced off the stage before turning back to the cameras. "It's time for a commercial break, but when we get back, we will continue this great conversation with Shafer McCartney—the Golden Ocelot. Stay tuned!"

And just like that, the first section ended. After the break, the rest of the interview continued in the same fashion as it had begun, with questions about Mission Omega, the limelight to which Shafer was suddenly exposed, personal life, and everything in between.

Finally, once he was finished, Shafer was dismissed backstage, where he was reunited with his aunt and Mr. Green, his recently assigned PR agent, who gave him a thumbs-up.

"That was mighty fine work, Shafer," Green said.
"You're lookin' like a natural."
"You taught me well."
He hugged his aunt, who held onto him a little tighter than normal. "You did great out there, Shafe," she whispered. I'm so proud of you."
"Thanks, June."
"And guess what?"
"What?"
"There's somebody here who wants to see you."
"Wait, what?"
"Surprise!" a familiar voice said from behind him.
Shafer let go of his aunt and spun around, coming face-to-face with May.
She threw her arms around him, burying her face into his shoulder. "I'm so happy to see you, Shafe!"
After a moment of babbling, Shafer found his voice. "May! I thought you weren't going to get here until tomorrow!"
"That was the plan, but your aunt thought it would be a nice surprise. I'm going to tag along until the reception tomorrow, and then you'll come with us."
"June, thank you." He let go of May with one arm only to wrap it back around his aunt. "You're the best."
"I know," his aunt said with a wink. "And I also know you've been missing May. But, for what it's worth, I kinda have been, too."
May giggled. "You did so well during the interview!"
"You watched it?"
"The whole thing. And hey... thanks for the shout-out."
He shrugged. "Apparently you have some competi-

tion on social media. That's what Emilia said."

She gently elbowed him in the ribs.

As he took her hand, Shafer exhaled and closed his eyes for a moment, trying to temporarily escape the relentless rush of action, lights, and attention. With this interview finished, for the next twenty-four hours, he could do whatever he wanted.

Mainly, he wanted to sleep. Since the end of Mission Omega, he hadn't slept in the same bed for consecutive nights, save the hospital bed during the first days of his recovery.

His aunt's voice brought him back to reality. "Are you ok, Shafe?"

"Huh?" He opened his eyes again, looking between June and May. "Oh, I'm great. I'm just… tired." He smiled at them, trying to be as convincing as possible.

"Are you sure? You need a break. You haven't been sleeping much, and you keep just going and going. It's getting ridiculous. You're gonna get sick."

"We're about done. One more day of this celebrity life, and then life will be back to the way it's always been."

"I'm not too sure about that," June argued, "but you will definitely be catching a break."

"And lots of sun," added May. "Are you packed for the trip?"

"Definitely not—I haven't even seen my house in two weeks," Shafer laughed. "But I'll get it done. I promise."

"Then let's get around and get back to the hotel," Mr. Green chimed in. "We can have you sleeping in your own bed tonight, Shafer."

Shafer squeezed May's hand. "If I get to see May and

my bed on the same day, I might just die of happiness."

"I'm not sure we can have that," May shot back. "I mean, at least get through the cruise first so the extra room we booked isn't wasted. Think you can do that?"

He grinned. "Deal. Let's leave this all behind. No more saving lives, just some time with you and your family."

"That sounds perfect."

THREE:
PRESIDENTIAL PARTY

Presidents belonged on TV, monuments, and even on money. They deserved to be *in* the spotlight, not shining it on a teenage boy.

But that's exactly what happened. President Warren Grady, microphone in hand, announced, "Ladies and gentlemen, put your hands together one more time for Mr. Shafer McCartney."

Thunderous applause accompanied the violent flash of cameras.

Shafer walked to the front of the stage, shook President Grady's hand, and then leaned forward so the president could drape a shiny, golden medal around his neck, just as they'd rehearsed this. But nothing was real anymore, or truly real, at least. Shafer's life was dictated by a script.

"Thank you, Shafer," President Grady spoke into

Shafer's ear, barely audible above the roar of the crowd. "I will leave you with the mic." He patted Shafer on the back, then walked to the back of the stage, sitting between two security guards.

Alone on the platform, Shafer looked out over a room full of people sitting at circular tables. They were all gazing back at him, waiting for him to speak. Political figures. Government agents. Maybe even some celebrities. He wasn't sure.

Shafer swallowed nervously. He couldn't find his voice.

Being interviewed by talk show hosts was nerve-wracking. Accepting an award from the President of the United States and giving a speech was even *worse*.

At a table close to the stage, he spotted his family and the Brimley's, along with Mr. Green. Kota, his best friend from D.C., sat beside his aunt and uncle. At the table beside him was Shafer's friend Murphy, who he had met during Mission Omega, and Murphy's parents.

A blonde woman caught Shafer's eye. She looked at the stage longingly, like she believed she should be elsewhere. Shafer also thought he recognized the man sitting beside her—perhaps it was her husband—but he seemed more interested in another woman beside him.

Mixed in among the crowd, reporters scribbled feverish notes or snapped pictures with canon-sized lenses. Shafer nervously gripped the medal around his neck as he eyed them. He'd practiced his speech several times, but now that the moment had finally arrived, he wasn't feeling very rehearsed.

Eventually, he stammered, "Thank you…" The mic wasn't picking him up well so he pulled it a little lower.

"Thank you all. For everything. This... this is too much." He felt inside the pocket of his blazer. He checked the other pocket. Then his pants pockets. Still, he felt nothing. He must have looked concerned. He could tell by the way his aunt was looking at him from the front row.

Shafer explained, "I... um... I had notes of what I wanted to say. Thank you's and stuff." After a moment more of searching, he gave up. "Apparently I lost those notes.... whoops."

There was a murmur of laughter from the audience.

"Guess I'm just going to shoot from the hip," he decided. "Seems fitting, though. That's pretty much how I got here."

Shafer tried to think back to the few notes he'd scrawled for his speech. "I promise I'm not gonna talk for long, *especially* without my notes, but I want to start with a few words of thanks." He looked back at the President. "First of all, I want to say a huge thank you to President Grady for this award. To have something like this named in my honor... there are no words, really."

This brought about a round of applause.

"I'd also like to thank God. He looks out for me, and honestly, I talked to Him a lot during everything that went down, lemme tell you. Also, God, I'm sorry for some of those choice words I said."

Another ripple of laughter.

"I want to thank my aunt and uncle. They've always treated me like their own son, and I love them. They've gotten me here."

More applause.

"I'd like to thank May Brimley because she is fantastic and really helped get me through Mission Omega. Same thing goes for Murphy. Thank you to everybody who checked on me while I was in the hospital, and a special thanks to Kota for keeping me entertained while I was there."

Shafer scanned the audience again. "I know I'm missing some people, and I'm sorry, but please know that I appreciate everyone that had any part in getting me here today."

That seemed inclusive enough, so he moved on. "I don't want to tell my story again. I've done that plenty over the past couple of weeks. Instead, I want to talk about something more important: dying."

A murmur came from the audience.

"I'm going somewhere with this, I promise." Shafer was trying to find the right words, going with his gut but deviating from any sort of speech he'd already planned out.

"After I was on Good Day USA yesterday, I got to thinking about something I'd said. To summarize, there was a time when I thought I was going to die at least six or seven times over twenty-four hours. I was chased by big cats, shot at by a hired militia, fell from a plane without a parachute, and got caught up in the middle of an army of robots. Oh, and there was a bomb, too."

There was more chuckling.

"And you know what I learned from all of it?" Shafer asked. "You gotta know what your priorities are. Make a conscious effort every single day to do that. For me, I didn't know what mattered most in my life until I was looking death in the face, over and over… and over. It's changed the way I live my life."

The crowd was silent, all eyes locked onto him.

"Since Mission Omega, every day for the past two weeks I have woken up, and the first coherent thought that pops into my mind is 'wow, I'm sure happy to be alive.' And if you think about it, that's the craziest thing—simply being alive is enough to put me in a great mood."

From across the audience, heads were nodding.

"But even more important is something else I realized," he went on. "I've learned that not only am I blessed to have a great life, but I also know that I could lose it at any given moment. If nothing else, my time with Blasnoff taught me that any given day could be my last."

After a slow look around the room, he declared, "That's why I have a challenge for you."

Placing one hand on the mic, he leaned in and said, "Don't forget that each moment could be your last. That makes the grass a little greener and the clouds a little whiter. Stop and smell the roses, then smell them again. Love your friends a lot, and love your family even more."

Heads nodded from across the audience, and he even saw a couple of people dabbing at their eyes.

"There's my challenge, and that's all I have to say. Thank you all so much, and I'm going to turn this back over to President Grady."

******

"My son is going to think this is the coolest thing ever. I'm pretty sure you're his favorite human being on the planet." The lady was talking anxiously as Shafer signed an 8x10 black-and-white picture of himself and handed it to her.

"That's awesome," he said. "Tell him we all have a little hero inside of us."

The woman nodded enthusiastically. "I'll tell him, Shafer. He'll love to hear that."

She stepped aside, and the next people in line moved up. This was a father and a grade-school-aged boy.

Shafer hated this. He'd been sitting at a table for nearly an hour and a half signing prints of himself labeled *First-Ever Recipient of the Shafer McCartney Medal of Heroism*. All the while, people drooled over him.

He felt like a circus animal more than anything. *Come see the spectacular Shafer McCartney, the savior of the world!* It was ridiculous. He smiled and made conversation, but the whole time he longed for it to be over.

And he didn't have a problem *meeting* the people. It was the way they treated him that he didn't like. He wanted to be their equal, their friend. They wanted him to be a god or something. How did celebrities—like *actual* celebrities—do this every day? Did they get numb to the limelight eventually?

He signed a print and took a picture with the boy before turning to a security guard behind him. "Hey, Frank, any idea how much longer I'm here?"

"Man, you've been at this for a while. I was told that you only had to go for thirty minutes."

"Wait, seriously?"

"Yeah, brother. F'real."

"You shoulda said something, man!" Shafer turned to see a little girl standing in front of the table. Her eyes seemed to plead for his attention.

"Sorry, Shafer. I assumed you knew."

Shafer shook his head, then asked, "How many more

people do you think are left? I can't tell from down here." He looked back to the little girl, whose worry-filled eyes seemed to beg for him not to go.

Frank rocked side-to-side, trying to see. "I don't know for sure, but I'd guess about two hundred."

"Two hundred?" Shafer sighed. He looked to the permanent marker in his hand, and then the girl in front of him. She didn't want to be the unlucky person who stood in line the whole time, just for him to call it quits before her turn.

And then, after the girl, the next boy would be the same way. Then the mother with the stroller. Then the man with the hat.

Shafer forced a smile at the girl and then asked Frank, "Could you go grab me a coffee? It sounds like we might be here for a while."

FOUR:
OFF THE GRID

"You've gotta be kidding me," was all Shafer could say as he looked up at the mansion before him.

"I stayed with you last night," May pointed out. "Don't act like your house isn't super nice."

"But... this is *huge*."

Mr. Brimley laughed as he climbed out of the driver's seat of his SUV. "That's the difference between living in residential Washington D.C. and rural Florida."

Shafer shook his head. "Stuart, you're the only person I've ever met in my life that calls beachfront property 'rural'."

Mr. Brimley grinned while opening the back hatch of his SUV.

"I think I might have overpacked," Shafer said, eyeing his two giant suitcases.

Mrs. Brimley looked over his shoulder. "It's always

better to have too much than not enough, sweetie."

"I guess, but this still seems like overkill..."

"Hello!" a voice came from behind Shafer.

He spun around. A man was walking up to them, dressed in khaki-colored overalls. He had intelligent eyes, greying hair, and kneepads strapped over his clothes. As he approached, he unfastened the pads and set them on the fresh-cut grass.

"Hey there," Mr. Brimley answered with confusion in his voice.

"I didn't mean to alarm you! I am Sylvio," the man continued, and this time Shafer picked up an Italian accent. "I'm the new groundsman. I've been working with Marco all morning, learning the ropes." Sylvio extended his hand, which Mr. Brimley shook.

"Wasn't my new groundsman... actually, never mind." Mr. Brimley shook his head. "It's been a crazy week and I can't keep anything straight. It's very nice to meet you, Sylvio. Happy to have you here."

"Yessir. Thank you, sir." Sylvio let go of Mr. Brimley's hand but held his gaze.

Sylvio didn't look like the average groundsman to Shafer, who had been around quite a few in the course of his life.

He was *dressed* the part, with his overalls sweaty from the humid Florida summer, but he didn't *look* the part. For one, Sylvio was much older than most—probably early fifties. With his sharp jaw, tanned skin, and well-kept beard, Sylvio seemed better-suited modeling for a cologne ad or alcohol commercial than trimming hedges.

Shafer turned away from the new groundsman and asked May, "Where should I take my bags?"

"Nonsense," Sylvio objected. "Allow me to carry them, young man."

"It's fine, really," Shafer said. "No worries."

"Please, I insist. It's what I'm here to do."

Shafer didn't want to cave completely, so he offered a compromise. "I'll tell you what. I have two bags and they're both gigantic, so I'll get one and you get the other." He gestured to the back of the SUV. "Your choice."

Sylvio grabbed the bigger of the two bags, and after Shafer took his duffel, the groundsman looked to him for instructions.

Shafer shrugged. "Um, I'm not sure where we're going. I'm new here, too. Sorry."

Mr. Brimley jumped in. "That's my fault! I should have introduced you. Sylvio, meet my wife, Heather, my daughter, May, and May's boyfriend, Shafer."

May and her mother waved, while Shafer, with his hands full, nodded.

"Shafer…" Sylvio said the name quietly and thoughtfully. "You look very familiar, Shafer."

"He gets that a lot," May joked without any further elaboration.

"It's very nice to meet you all," Sylvio replied. "I've heard wonderful things about your family and I'm very thankful for this job."

"We're thankful to have you," Mr. Brimley replied. "But you two don't need to stand around with that heavy luggage. Please, follow me."

With that, Shafer was led into the Brimley's home.

While Shafer had grown up in a very nice home, this one was much larger and had a lot more extravagant details, from the white-marble walkway to the porch that wrapped around the entire house, to the tremendous living room on the first floor that overlooked crystal-clear ocean water lapping against a white beach that was basically in the backyard.

As he followed Mr. Brimley through the house in a trance, it was all he could do not to stare. "Your home is amazing, Stuart," he said.

"Thank you, Shafer," Mr. Brimley answered. "It's been a fun project for two decades, something we've enjoyed tweaking and changing." He waved toward his wife. "Heather's the brains behind it, though. I can't take much credit."

"Really?" Shafer looked at Mrs. Brimley.

She playfully rolled her eyes. "We both came up with some ideas, but I do have a background in architecture, though."

"Really?" He asked. "So did you design the blueprints for the house?"

"I helped with the first draft, yes. But from there I just watched everything unfold."

"So have you worked in architecture before? I know this seems silly, but I don't really know what you do."

"I work for Edge with Stuart. I'm a part-time company photographer."

"Photographer? What do you take pictures of?"

"Employees, mainly. Sometimes happy customers and deals being made. Things for the website and newsletter."

"Oh, that makes a lot of sense. I bet there's a lot to see at headquarters!"

"Absolutely. And HQ is just about forty minutes from here. We can go tomorrow if you'd like to see it, right Stu?"

Mr. Brimley grinned. "I'll have to let security know we'll have a VIP on the premises, but yes, I'd love to show you Edge."

"Don't get too excited, Shafe," scoffed May. "My parents act like it's cool, but it's mainly nerdy-looking people sitting around and staring at computer monitors. And I'm talking about the kinds of people that have to calculate responses when you speak to them."

"I'm sure it will be fun."

Mr. Brimley said, "This way. We're going to the second floor."

Shafer headed towards the stairs against the far wall.

Mr. Brimley stopped him. "Actually, let's take the elevator."

"Oh, yeah." Shafer paused, caught slightly off-guard. "That makes sense."

Mrs. Brimley headed to the kitchen while Shafer, Mr. Brimley, May, and Sylvio rode the elevator upstairs. They ascended in silence until Mr. Brimley asked, "So, Sylvio, where are you from?"

Sylvio, still clutching the suitcase with a steely grip, answered, "Italy, originally, but my parents immigrated to California when I was ten."

"Oh, you've gone coast-to-coast," Mr. Brimley said. "How long have you been in Florida? Can I ask what brought you here?"

Ding. The elevator reached the second floor and the doors slid open. Shafer exited with the rest of the group following him.

"Nine months," Sylvio said. "Love it here. Unfortunately, I came here to take care of my mother, who is ill."

"Oh…" Mr. Bimley looked uncomfortable. "I'm very sorry. I didn't mean to pry. Please let me know if there's anything I can do."

Sylvio shook his head. "It is no problem, sir. Like I said, I'm just flattered for the opportunity to work for you. Making a little extra money will help take care of things at home. I thought I was retired, but circumstances can somehow bring you right back in the thick of things."

As Shafer followed them down a long hall, he asked, "What did you retire from, if I can ask?"

"I was an EMT," Sylvio answered. "An exciting job, for sure. Very rewarding, but sometimes very sad."

"I can imagine. I bet you've seen a lot of things."

"Certainly, sir."

"Guys, this is the room," Mr. Brimley steered them through a doorway on the right side of the hall. "Shafer, this will be yours for the next couple days."

"Oh wow, thank you!" Shafer set his bag on the floor beside his bed and walked to the window, looking out at the same ocean-front view. As he watched the frothy ocean roll up to land, he said, "Your backyard is a private beach."

"You and May can do some swimming," Mr. Brimley replied. "If you think of anything you need in your room, please let me know. The shower and bathroom are just through there." He pointed.

May smirked. "I hate to break it to you, Shafe, but the mirror on your dresser here doesn't talk to you."

"Oh, thank the Lord. I don't want any reminders of Blasnoff's castle of horrors," Shafer said with a forced laugh.

A confused Mr. Brimley was quickly filled in on what

May had been referencing, and when they were finished, he chuckled and said, "Yeah, we don't have any smart mirrors in the house, Shafer, but I can promise that nobody here wants to kill you, at least."

Shafer smirked. "That's a trade-off I'll take any day of the week."

Sylvio placed Shafer's suitcase beside the duffle and politely excused himself, saying he had to get back to work.

Mr. Brimley put his hand on May's shoulder. "Let Shafer get unpacked then show him the layout of the house. I've gotta call Anthony and put out a few work-related fires, then I'll help your mom with dinner."

"You're supposed to be off, remember?" May scolded.

"I know, but nobody told Amazon that they should leave us alone for a week, and I have to just send an analytic report. Ten minutes—tops."

"Good. Love you."

"Love you, too," Mr. Brimley began to leave, but another figure arrived at the door.

"Mr. Brimley, welcome home!" Much like Sylvio, this voice had an accent as well, but a Spanish one.

"Marco, thank you." Mr. Brimley stepped to the side so a second man could enter the room. "Marco, this is Shafer McCartney, May's boyfriend. Shafer, this is Marco, the best groundsman to ever walk the earth. He's worked for me for nearly twenty years."

Shafer extended his hand. "It's a pleasure to meet you."

"No," Marco replied. "The pleasure is all mine. I've heard about everything you've been through, Shafer. Not only from May, but from yourself, too! On TV, I mean."

"Thanks. It's been pretty crazy, for sure."

Marco sympathetically bobbed his head. "Then it sounds like your trip will suit you well. You need a break, and I know Stuart does too. And speaking of…" He reached inside his shirt pocket and pulled out a small, shiny object. "Guess what arrived this morning?"

Mr. Brimley reached out and took the object, a flash of excitement on his face. "You don't say? I didn't even see the notification. Thank you for taking care of it, Marco."

"You're welcome."

"It sounds like you've had a busy morning with our new groundsman."

Marco nodded. "Definitely. But Sylvio has been a lot of help. A quick learner, for sure."

Shafer managed to identify the object that Marco had handed Mr. Brimley: a car key.

At the same time, Mr. Brimley turned to him and May. "It was about time to upgrade, so I just bought a new car. I guess it arrived this morning."

Shafer asked, "They brought it here? You didn't have to go to a car lot?"

"I scheduled it for delivery, yes," Mr. Brimley answered. "To be honest, I haven't seen it in person yet. But I think it's going to be quite the beauty."

"Oh, it is," agreed Marco.

Mr. Brimley looked at the teenagers. "What do you say? Shall we go check it out?"

Shafer nodded eagerly while May shrugged.

"Eh, that's about the reaction I expected from her," Mr. Brimley joked. "Did you park it in the garage, Marco?"

Marco shook his head. "No sir. I didn't want to take the first drive. It's just beside the house where they unloaded it."

"Thank you, Marco." Mr. Brimley turned to Shafer. "Can you wait to unpack for a bit?"

"Oh yes. I love cars. I just gotta plug in my phone—it's almost dead."

"The outlet's right there."

They headed back outside, and it turned out that the house was no more impressive than the car parked on the driveway: a brand new Maserati sports car, candy-apple red with white trim.

Shafer nearly began to drool on sight. "Whoa! This is *sick*. This car..." He trailed off. "It's incredible. You did well, Mr. Brim... *Stuart*."

Mr. Brimley walked over to the car, unlocked it, and peered inside. "I liked what I read online. It's a V8, 484 horsepower, and goes zero-to-sixty in 2.4 seconds. They said it can do a one-eighty. Can you imagine?"

"Are you... are you gonna try it out?"

"Oh heavens, no. I'm too old for that." Mr. Brimley chuckled. "But the power is impressive. It's a smooth ride, too, supposedly."

From behind them, the garage door opened and Mrs. Brimley came outside. Her expression looked almost identical to May's as she said, "I at least like this one better than the one you sold."

Peeping over the top of the car, Mr. Brimley had a boyish grin on his face. "What do you like about it, hon?"

"The color."

"Oh..."

DELTA ADRIFT

Shafer followed May over to the car but couldn't help but feel intimidated as he approached, like he shouldn't even breathe near this beauty of a machine. He was used to the black SUVs his uncle had driven since Shafer was in diapers. This sports car seemed like it should be in a museum—it was *art*.

And that's why Shafer's heart raced when Mr. Brimley said, "Climb in, Shafer. You too, May."

It was an offer he couldn't refuse, but when Shafer began to walk to the passenger side of the car, Mr. Brimley stopped him. "No, Shafer. Not what I meant."

Confused, Shafer turned back around, only for Mr. Brimley to extend his hand and press the car key into his palm. "I want you to do the honors."

"Me…?" Shafer nearly choked on his tongue. "I couldn't. I appreciate it, but…"

"No, I *insist*." Mr. Brimley pointed at May. "Go with him."

"Where are we supposed to go?" she asked.

"I was thinking *Lucky's*."

"Ice cream? Before dinner?" Mrs. Brimley objected at first but then paused. "Wait, that was *our* first date. Aw, that's sweet, Stu."

Mr. Brimley shrugged, grinning again. "Sheer coincidence, certainly." He wore a knowing look on his face as he first looked at his wife, then May and Shafer. "I trust you guys. Just take it easy. If you can save the world, you can drive that car too, Shafer."

Shafer didn't know what to say, so he simply nodded, almost trance-like.

Fortunately, May shook him out of it, pinching him on the arm. "What are you waiting for? Take me on a date, Shafe."

Shafer turned to Mr. and Mrs. Brimley, thanking them with his eyes since his mouth had apparently broken, then climbed into the driver's seat of the brand new luxury sports car. With May beside him and his heart racing, he gripped the steering wheel, nodded to Mr. Brimley, and started the car.

FIVE:
ACCELERATE

As the car rolled forward, Shafer glanced at May in the passenger seat beside him. She was beautiful, with her flowing blonde hair and her bright smile. And she was laughing. Laughing at *him*. "Don't look so nervous," she said.

Shafer shook his head. "May, this car is *insane*. I can't believe your dad let me drive it. In fact, he might be insane, too!"

"He adores you." May rolled her eyes playfully. "Not even kidding, you're all he's talked about for the last couple of weeks. I'm pretty sure he wouldn't let *me* drive the new car, but Shafer McCartney? Oh, of course."

Shafer caressed the steering wheel delicately. "That's just because you don't appreciate the beauty of this car."

"Yeah, yeah. As long as it gets me where I want to go, that's all I care about."

"What do you drive, anyway?"

She pointed out the window as they drove forward. "The van parked to the far left."

Shafer followed her finger to the four-car garage, which had an empty spot for the new Maserati, and he located the van she was talking about. It was pale blue, definitely not new, not fancy, and certainly not what he expected.

He couldn't help himself. "May, you drive a straight-up soccer-mom van."

"Hey! It's what they gave me, and it works." After a moment, she added, "My dad said that I wouldn't appreciate a nice car unless I started with something like that."

Shafer shrugged. "Okay, I admire that. Your dad's a good guy."

"Wow. The way you talk about each other... You'd make a cute couple."

He grinned. "Greatness appreciates greatness, I guess." For a brief moment he wanted to reach out and take May's hand, but he was also scared to death to take one of his hands off of the steering wheel as they neared the edge of the driveway. "So where are we going?"

"*Lucky's,*" she answered. "It's this cute little bakery with gourmet ice cream. It's been in town for longer than I've been alive."

"I meant like... where do I turn?"

"Oh!" May pointed. "Turn right here, and we'll follow the road for a while. They also make this really fancy device called a GPS that—"

"Yeah, yeah, I got it," Shafer cut her off as he signaled, an unfamiliar clicking sound in the new car. Once he pulled through the gate at the end of the driveway, he checked both ways about four times before turning out on the road, and with that, they were off.

The horsepower of the vehicle was incredible. Even the slightest tap on the gas pedal was enough to rev it up, and it took a conscious effort not to go from twenty miles-per-hour to sixty as he was trying to get up to speed.

He was sitting low, too. The two-door sports car was much lower on the ground than anything else he had ever driven before, and he couldn't help but feel like he was nearly dragging his leather seat against the concrete. As he gained speed, his heart rate once again started to rise.

"What's the speed limit?" he asked May.

She was leaning against the tinted window, gazing out into the afternoon light. "Forty-five. But like, we never see any highway patrol back here if you want to go faster."

Shafer adamantly shook his head. "No chance. We'll be doing at least five-under the entire trip."

"You're the guy who fights robots. Don't tell me you're scared to drive sixty."

"This is like a hundred-thousand-dollar car, maybe more, and it's not even *mine*," Shafer insisted. "And something tells me that your dad didn't pay to have me on the insurance plan."

May playfully sighed. "Well, if one of us *were* on it, it'd be you."

"That's because you'd speed in the new Maserati." With an open road, no traffic, and feeling a little braver, Shafer reached out and put his hand on her knee. "May?"

"Yes?"

"I'm really glad to be here with you."

"Aw, Shafer. Me too."

He anxiously put his hand back on the wheel as they rounded a curve. "Think about it. How much time have we spent with each other since everything happened?"

"I mean... just a little."

"Yeah, not much. And none alone, just us. I think this is the first time we've been able to spend time by ourselves since... I don't even remember."

May was quiet for just a moment. "You're right. I hadn't thought of that. It's nice to be able to just relax, breathe, and enjoy each other's company."

Shafer grinned. "That's coming from the person *not* driving the six-figure car, so I'll take that with a grain of salt."

May shot him a look before they both burst into laughter.

It was a laugh of relief. Of joy. Of happiness that they were on their own, free to explore and free to ignore the needs and desires of anybody else. There were no more pictures, no more interviews, none of that. Just Shafer, May, and the open road.

May reached out and patted Shafer on the arm. "I'm proud of you, Shafe. About time you stop driving like a grandpa."

She was right. The car was going faster now and he hadn't even realized he was speeding up. As the trees whizzed past, Shafer shook his head. "Don't worry—I wasn't trying to. I guess I just got a little excited. It doesn't take much to get this thing moving." He moved his foot to the brake and tapped it.

Nothing happened.

"Um... May?"

DELTA ADRIFT

"What's up, Vin Diesel?"

Shafer stepped on the brake again, this time with a lot more force. Still, the car didn't respond. He glanced at the speedometer, which was registering fifty-five miles per hour.

"The... the brakes aren't working."

"What?" She leaned over, staring at the high-tech dashboard. "Did you set it on cruise control?"

"I mean, that wouldn't turn off the brakes." He pressed the cruise control button on the steering wheel, making sure it was off. "Yeah, that's not it."

"Then what's wrong? Is there some secret to driving one of these things?"

"I was hoping you could tell me."

"Dad gave *you* the keys."

Shafer shook his head, glancing from the road back to the dashboard. "I... I don't see anything." He stomped the brake into the spotless floorboard, but nothing happened. "Call your dad."

"Already on it." May was lifting her phone to her ear, but then pressed a button and put it on speaker.

It only rang twice before Mr. Brimley picked it up. "Hey, you guys ok?"

"Hey, Dad." May held the phone to her mouth. "This car... how do you slow it down?"

"Um, what do you mean?" Mr. Brimley sounded confused. "There are two pedals on the floor. One is the gas, the other is the brake, and..."

"No, we get *that*," May couldn't keep the annoyance out of her voice. "Not the time for bad dad jokes."

"What's going on then?"

"The brakes aren't working! Shafer is stepping on the

brake, and nothing is happening." There was silence on the other end. "Dad? Dad, what's wrong with the car? What do we do?"

After a moment, a slow response came. "I... I don't know. Has Shafer pressed any buttons by accident?" He sounded concerned, but also like he was trying very hard *not* to sound concerned.

"I haven't," Shafer said. "My hands are at ten and two. I'm not used to fancy sports cars, but I don't think I've done anything to make it do... well, this."

"I'm heading to my truck," Mr. Brimley responded. Then, in the background, he yelled out, "Heather, come here. Grab your phone."

"What do we do?" May's voice was growing shakier as she repeated the question. "I think your car has a mind of its own."

Over the phone, Mr. Brimley's truck door slammed as he gave instructions to his wife. "Call the police. Something's wrong with the car and the kids can't get it to slow down."

There was a loud exclamation from Mrs. Brimley, then, from what Shafer could make out, she said, "What do you mean? What do I..."

"We're going to follow them. Just call 9-1-1 and tell them what's going on and where." Back to Shafer and May, he asked, "How fast are you guys going?"

"About fifty-five," Shafer answered, but as his eyes glanced back to the dashboard, he realized this was no longer the case. "Scratch that. We're doing sixty-six."

May chimed in with, "Sixty-six? What the hell..."

The speedometer continued to creep up. "I don't know what's going on," Shafer stammered, "but we're gaining speed. I'm not touching the gas, but..." He trailed off as he looked back to the road, which lazily curved to the right. Tropical trees hugged the shoulder on both sides, thick enough that it was hard to see too far ahead.

He checked the speed again. "We, uh... we just hit seventy."

A blue car rounded the corner ahead of them. Shafer swore, hugging the curb as tightly as possible, and as the road wound back to the left, it was everything he could to keep from drifting into the other lane and hitting the car.

The driver, a sunglasses-wearing woman with frizzy blonde hair, laid on her horn with profanity on her lips.

"What was that?" Mr. Brimley asked.

"We just rounded a curb doing 70 and almost crunched somebody," May stammered. Shafer, with his breath held, was too focused to even speak.

"Yeah, there's definitely something wrong with the car," Mr. Brimley concluded. "We're on the way. Where are you guys?"

May pointed to an exit up ahead and said, "Turn there Shafer."

"The entrance ramp to the interstate?"

"This road only gets curvier, so if we stay the course we're gonna end up impaled on a tree. Do you want that?"

"Fair point. The interstate sounds good to me." Shafer signaled.

To her father, May said, "We're about to get onto I-95."

"I-95?" Mr. Brimley's voice wavered.

"Yeah, we can't do the backroads at this speed." May pointed out the windshield. "Watch out for the toll booth."

"Yeah, I see it." He held his breath and gritted his teeth as they blew past it. The astonished woman inside flashed them a look.

"Thank God there wasn't a car there," he muttered. "Stuart, we just hit eighty."

Mr. Brimley quickly relayed the information to Mrs. Brimley, who was talking to the police in the background. He then said, "There's got to be something you can try... Shafer, can you put the car in neutral?"

As he sped up the entrance ramp, Shafer peered over his shoulder to make sure he was. "I can try in just a sec. I'm trying to merge."

The traffic was not too bad, so as soon as he managed to work into the flow, he tried to do as Mr. Brimley had said. "Nothing. It won't budge."

"Press on the brake and try again."

"My foot hasn't *left* the brake, I promise. Um... any other ideas?"

"Can you kill the engine?"

This gave Shafer a spark of hope, and he reached forward and twisted on the key, but it didn't budge. "No luck..."

While May went back and forth with her father, trying to relay anything that her mom could usefully pass on to the police, Shafer had to block out the conversation just to focus on the task at hand: driving well enough to stay alive.

The surrounding traffic had other ideas. Even on the interstate, Shafer was moving considerably faster than everybody else, so his only choice was to weave around the vehicles as he came upon them. He blew past a white truck, which honked angrily, but by that point, Shafer was driving fast enough that he was almost out of earshot before the honk even ended.

He couldn't keep this up forever. One wrong move would be all it took for him and May to go slamming into the back of a vehicle.

His knuckles were white and he was barely breathing. He'd played games like this on his PlayStation, but in real life, it was no fun at all. There was only one way for this to end unless he figured something out *very* soon.

"Ah, great." It was all he could say as he suddenly saw a police car ahead of him in the middle lane of the interstate. "This is gonna go well."

He wasn't sure which happened first: blowing by the police car or seeing its lights flash on in a blaze of red and blue. The squad car began to pursue, but it struggled to keep up.

May, looking over her shoulder, asked, "Shafer, um... how fast are we going now?"

Shafer was almost afraid to look, and once he did, he regretted it. "One-eleven."

"*Are you kidding?*"

"I wish."

Holding the phone back up, May shouted to her father, "We're doing one-eleven and just passed a squad car, so if Mom hasn't alerted the police yet, we took care of it for you." She was fighting to keep back tears. "Dad, what do we do?"

"Dammit," Shafer swore as he spotted brake lights ahead of him.

"We're gonna die!" May exclaimed. "Shafer!"

"Hold on!" Gritting his teeth, Shafer skidded over to the shoulder of the road. Tires squealing, the Maserati vibrated so intensely that it felt like it might explode. Shafer did everything in his power just to keep it from drifting into the concrete barricade to his left.

May screamed. Shafer might have even screamed, too, but he wasn't sure. But what mattered the most was that he managed to keep the car on the road, then somehow coax it back into the traffic lane.

Hands shaking, he moved over the middle lane, desperately scanning the traffic in front of him. "Any other ideas, May?"

"Don't hit anything."

Seconds felt like decades as they ticked by. All the while, the Maserati kept accelerating. By the time they hit one-hundred and thirty miles per hour, Shafer could barely see anything around him. They were moving so fast that the surrounding world was a blur. All he could do was look straight ahead.

There were two ways Shafer could imagine slowing down the car: running out of gas or slamming it into something. Obviously, the first option was a lot more favorable than the second, but with a nearly-full tank of gas, the second was much more likely.

May's attempt at conversation with her father had turned into more whimpers and sobs than actual words, and Shafer was feeling the same way. He was playing with borrowed time at this point, and when May finally managed to put together half a sentence, it was the nail in the coffin.

"Shafer, are those... brake lights?" The words were damning, a one-way ticket to his funeral.

She was right. Up ahead, for one reason or another, traffic had come to a standstill. All the lanes were full of cars, nobody was moving, and there was nowhere to go but into either the back of a car or the concrete barriers around the road.

"Dad, I love you," May yelled into her phone between sobs. "Traffic is stopped.... I love you and Mom."

"May..." It was almost hard to hear Mr. Brimley's response over the roar of the car's engine and the whoosh of the atmosphere around them. "May, I love you too."

Shafer, meanwhile, hoped for two things: immediate death was the first, and the other was that he wouldn't kill anybody else along the way. He'd aim the Maserati-torpedo for the concrete barrier along the road and pray that nobody else would be injured in the fallout. It was what he had to do. It was the responsible thing.

Unless...

Out of the corner of his eye, he noticed an exit ramp. "Where does that go?" he asked, but immediately realized *regardless* of where it went, it had to be better than where he was headed.

So Shafer made a move. He jerked on the steering wheel and sharply veered the car across the interstate and toward the exit ramp, earning more honks from every direction. Before he was even halfway across, they began to skid, and for a moment he was sure he'd never make it...

But he did. By inches, at that.

May cried, Shafer swore, and together they flew down the exit ramp so fast that the car lifted off the ground for a moment.

However, it didn't take long to shift from one problem to the next. At the bottom of the ramp was a road sign. *Detour,* it read, with a giant arrow pointing to the right. Another sign beside it explained: *Road closed. Bridge construction.*

Shafer had never been a great student in physics class, but as he looked at the detour and the roadblock ahead of him, he knew there was no way he was going to get the car turned in time. Whether the road was closed or not, they would be taking it. It was the only choice.

"Shafer... what are you doing?" Maybe gasped.

"Hold on!" Ignoring the traffic sign, he kept the car driving straight. They knifed right through the reflective traffic barricade, jarring the car as it plowed over plastic cones, and blazed down the closed road.

"On the bright side," Shafer mumbled, "we're not going to run into any traffic here."

"May?" Mr. Brimley's voice yelled from the phone's speaker. "May, what happened? Please tell me you're okay."

"For now," May shakily answered. "We got off the interstate. We're on a closed road."

"Why is it closed?"

"Bridge construction," she replied. "Let's hope the bridge is okay."

Shafer's eyes widened as he spotted something out his front windshield. "Yeah, that bridge is *not* okay."

"What do you mean?" Mr. Brimley sounded desperate. "Shafer?"

May gasped. "The bridge... it's gone."

Shafer checked the speedometer. They were going one-hundred and forty-six miles-per-hour downhill, headed to the void of a bridge that had been completely demolished.

This was it.

There was no going back, no slowing, and no turning around.

But he spotted something that, for the first time in a while, gave him hope. Water. He couldn't tell how deep it was, but water—an inlet from the ocean—glistened in the afternoon light at the bottom of the ravine ahead of them.

"Stuart," he said through gritted teeth as he fought to keep the car aimed at the ramp, "I think I'm about to get your car a lil' wet."

"What do you mean? Where are you guys?"

May was piecing together what Shafer had in mind and she stammered, "No way… no way. Shafer, you're not ramming the car into the ocean, right?"

They closed in on the ramp. "Sounds a lot better than ramming it into a tree, doesn't it?"

"We're gonna die," May said again. "Dad, I love you. Mom too. You're the best parents I could have ever asked for… We are *definitely* gonna die."

"No, we're not," Shafer insisted. "Just hold on. This might be a rough landing."

Before they could get out another word, they reached the end of the road, raced up it, and the car, along with two screaming teenagers, soared into the air.

SIX:
SUNKEN

The impact was jarring.
When the flying Maserati crashed into the surface of the water, the airbag deployed with a blast. Then, for the first time since Shafer had pulled out of the Brimley's driveway, the engine stopped running.

"May," he called out, "are you okay?"

No response.

"May?" As he fought the airbag out of his face and looked her way, he saw the last thing he wanted to see: May's head was slouched to the side, leaning against the window. The crash had knocked her out cold.

"No... May." He shoved the airbag out of his way and then wrestled her loose. *Where was her phone?* She'd been holding it when they crashed, and with any luck, Mr. Brimley might still be on the other end of the line.

He checked in her lap. He checked the seat beside her. Growing desperate, he unfastened his seatbelt so he could look more extensively. Finally, he spotted it, lying face-down on the floorboard right under her seat.

But, as he looked for the phone, the light flickered. He squinted, rubbing his eyes, but nothing changed—the space around him was going darker.

Soon, he understood why. Water was rising up the glass of the windshield as the car began to sink. The light faded even more.

Before long, they'd be completely submerged.

Shafer desperately reached out, slipping his hand under the tight space of the seat, only to make another discovery. The floorboard was wet. More than wet, even. It was *soaked*. Water was pooling in the car.

He reached further until his fingertips were on the phone. "Stuart," he yelled out. "Stuart, can you hear me?"

There was no reply, which wasn't a good sign, but soon Shafer understood why. When he pulled May's phone from under the seat, he found that the screen was covered with a spider web of cracks. Water ran from the phone, dripping off his elbow.

"Dammit," he muttered as the light continued fading away. By now they were sunk, fully submerged below the surface.

And that's when the floodgates burst open. Or, in this case, the air vents. The pressure of the water outside had grown strong enough that water began blasting through them with so much force that he had to move so it wasn't beating into his chest. The water filling the small car was already up to Shafer's shins.

He leaned over toward May to push her slumped body from in front of the blast. "May, wake up." Shafer slapped her cheeks desperately. "May, I really need you to

come out of it."
Her head continued to droop.
"May, wake up! I need your help. Please!"
Still nothing.
"Why does this kinda stuff always happen to me?" Shafer grumbled. If May wasn't waking up he was going to have to do this on his own, and that was going to be nearly impossible. "May?"
More frantic, he reached over and unhooked her seatbelt, pulling her free from it.
The water worked its way to his knees as the car continued to sink.
It was dark enough that he was straining to see, so much of his movement was based on feel. As the water reached his waist, an even bigger concern came to mind: if May was unconscious, she wouldn't know to hold her breath. *That's how it worked, right?* Even if he could get her loose and swim with her to the surface, she'd probably drown in the process.
"May, I *really* need you to wake up," he yelled, but there was still no response.
He only had one option: he had to seal her airways.
As the water gurgled up to his ribs, he reached over with one arm and wrapped it around her, covering her mouth with his palm and pinching her nose between his thumb and pointer finger.
He was suffocating her now, but it had to be done. Her body wasn't getting any oxygen, but it also wasn't going to take on any water. Still, how long could he do this to her? How long could she go without breathing? Thirty seconds? Maybe forty-five? Every second could mean life or death for them both.

DELTA ADRIFT

"For a first real date, this really sucks," he muttered, but the words rattled emptily in the car as it continued to sink deeper in the dark depths of the ocean.

Readjusting his grip on May, Shafer pulled on the door handle, prepared to swim out of the car with his girlfriend.

It didn't budge.

What the hell? He tried again, but only to achieve the same result. It was unlocked—he was sure of that—so why wasn't it opening?

He looked back to the water blasting through the air vents, and suddenly, the answer struck him: Pressure. Since the car was completely underwater, the water outside was forcing its way in—so much so that the unequal pressure clamped the door shut. Try as he might, there was no way he was going to get it to budge until the car was entirely full of water and the pressure balanced out.

He looked at the driver's side window, contemplating breaking it with his elbow. That would be his quickest way out, but there was no way he'd be able to pull May through the window after him. She'd surely drown.

He was left with one option.

He had to wait.

And it was the longest wait of his life. As the water continued to rise, Shafer temporarily took his hand off May's face, allowing her to take in the air. The water was chest-level now, gurgling higher with every passing second.

If the car had to be completely full of water for him to open the door, he had at least another thirty seconds to wait.

How deep were they? He leaned forward, the water

from the vents pounding his chest. Through the windshield, he could see the surface glinting somewhere above them, but he couldn't tell whether it was twenty feet or sixty feet away.

Since May's unconscious body was now neck-deep in water, the reduced gravity made her a lot easier to move. He pulled her out of the seat and turned her face towards the roof, sitting her on the console between the two seats to elevate her head as much as possible.

In the meantime, he accidentally caught a mouthful of salty ocean water and coughed, trying to catch his breath as the water level reached his neck.

"I don't know if you can hear me, May," he said, "But I'm gonna get you out of here. I'm going to swim you to the surface, and you won't be able to breathe, but just hang in there. *Please.* You've gotta trust me."

The water reached his jawline and he extended his head, taking one last big breath as he wrapped an arm under May's shoulder and then once again sealed off her airways.

And with that, the water filled the car. The rush fell silent as the vents began to let up, and a final bubble rolled out of each of them, bursting against the ceiling of the car.

This was it. They were completely submerged. No more air— or not down here, at least. If Shafer wanted to take another breath, he was going to have to work for it, and he was going to have to take some dead weight along for the trip.

Clutching onto May, he tried the door.

To his relief, it swung open.

Just like he'd scripted in his mind, he pulled May out

of the car, careful to keep his hand clamped on her face. Once outside, he scanned his surroundings. The car had come to rest on a sandy shelf in the middle of the ocean, but they had been lucky—another fifteen feet farther and the car would have been sinking down a dropoff into the deep blue abyss.

But that was the extent of his luck, because fixing his eyes overhead, the surface looked farther than Shafer had thought. It was going to be quite the swim.

He didn't have a moment to waste, so he had to get moving. Tightening his grip on May, he crouched down against the sandy seafloor, tightened the muscles in his legs, and pushed off to the surface.

It was excruciating.

He kicked and paddled, stroked and lurched, fought and reached, and for a moment Shafer was sure they were going to be okay, that he could make it. Then, all at once, the crippling, breathless exhaustion hit him and his oxygen-starved body refused to cooperate. It refused to push any further.

And down he went. With May in one arm and the other desperately clawing up toward the surface, Shafer began to sink. Her weight was pulling him down, and he couldn't stop it. He couldn't save her.

His vision went blurry from the lack of oxygen and the sting of the saltwater. His pulse pounded in his ears and his lungs burned in his chest. His choices seemed resoundingly clear: He either had to let May go and he would live, or else they were both going to die. He'd drown trying to save her.

And still, he couldn't let go. He couldn't watch her body float away, disappearing back into the depths. If he did that, he wouldn't be able to live with himself anyway.

Shafer squinted his eyes shut and kicked. Not an aggressive kick, either, just enough to stay afloat. Enough to hold his position.

By now, both his lungs and brain were screaming for air. His instincts told him to take a deep breath, but if he did that here, he would ingest nothing but water, choke, and drown. It was a claustrophobic, helpless feeling, and he didn't know what to do.

But he had to try.

While he kicked and maintained, he'd managed to collect just enough energy for one last push. One final desperate attempt to reach the surface. He forced his eyes open again, peering up at the surface, and with a glance down at May, he took off.

At first, his legs burned as badly as his lungs, but then they went numb. All the feeling left them as the oxygen fled from his body. His lungs were suffocating. His brain was shutting down. His vision was fleeting.

Yet he pushed on. He kicked purposefully, covering as much ground as he could while making every stroke count, and just when Shafer was sure he was going to suffocate, he burst from the depths, out of the water, and into the air.

It was the biggest, sweetest breath of oxygen he'd ever taken in his life.

And then, after he took another breath and managed to collect his thoughts as his brain reoxygenated, he took care of May. She needed the air just as much as he did, if not more, so he freed her airways and held her above the water, focusing enough on doing so that he once again dipped below the surface for a moment.

"Breathe, May," he told her as he resurfaced. "Get some air, because we're not out of this yet."

She offered no response, but he gave her ample time to take in some air before he began paddling forward once again, covering her face as he swam them to the shore.

This swim was just as tiring as the first because it was a much longer distance, but thankfully, this time he could take breaks to catch his breath along the way. May's weight kept pulling him down, and twice he wondered if he'd be able to truly make it all the way, but soon, his feet were striking the sandy bottom of the ocean floor.

Finally able to stand, he pulled May into him, leaning her over his shoulder, and trudged through the sand, heading toward the beach.

There was a cliff in front of him, and at the top of it he could see a few metal beams that used to be part of the now-missing bridge.

"In hindsight, I guess I was lucky that the bridge *wasn't* there," he panted as he began to climb out of the water. His eyes stung and his mouth tasted salty, but he was safe. He was alive.

Now he just had to worry about May, who was still unresponsive.

Suddenly he heard a voice shout, "There they are!" To his right, he spotted a handful of people that began running down an overgrown walking trail that led to the beach. Mr. Brimley was leading the charge, flanked by his sobbing wife and four police officers. He was pointing at Shafer.

The physical exhaustion weighed on Shafer enough that as soon as he made it out of the water, he dropped to his knees. May was still on his shoulder, so he took care to lay her down fully out of the water, positioning her on the sand. Her chest continued to rise and fall but her eyes remained closed.

Mr. Brimley took off in a run, sprinting toward them with his wife at his heels.

As they approached, Mrs. Brimley cried out. "Shafer, is she..." The words were barely intelligible through her sobs.

Shafer tried to respond, but he didn't even have the energy to muster up words yet. After a couple more deep breaths, he managed, "She's breathing, but she got knocked out on impact with the water." He turned his attention to her. "May? May, can you hear me? Wake up, May."

In a matter of seconds, one of the policemen was kneeling beside Shafer. He checked her for a pulse before confirming, "she's alive, but she must have lots of water in her lungs."

"No," Shafer wheezed. "I made sure of it. I held her mouth and nose shut until the car flooded, then I pulled her to the surface." He continued shaking her, gently but firmly. As the seconds ticked past, desperation crept in.

Mrs. Brimley collapsed down beside Shafer, throwing her arms around him. "Shafer..." It was all she could say at first before she joined Shafer in trying to wake May, begging for her to open her eyes or offer up any kind of sign that she was okay.

As Shafer watched, longing for a response that refused to come, he couldn't help but feel tears welling up in his eyes. What if, despite his best efforts, he hadn't done enough? What if she'd suffered brain damage from the asphyxiation? What if she was never going to wake up?

While those thoughts coursed through his mind, the other three officers were taking action. One checked May's vitals while the other two shared their location with more emergency personnel.

A mustached officer said, "The ambulance will be here within minutes. Can we get her to the road?"

"We should leave her here and wait on a stretcher," the first officer replied. "We'll…"

"Shafer?" At first, Shafer had thought the soft voice saying his name was that of Mrs. Brimley, but he was wrong. It was *May*. Hearing her say his name made his heart leap in his chest.

"May!" He grabbed her by the hand while Mrs. Brimley shouted out praises and took her arm.

"Shafer…" May said again, and this time her eyes were lazily fluttering open. "You saved me, Shafer."

He didn't have the words to express his relief, so he wrapped his arms around her and pulled her close.

"Stay here ma'am," 'Stache said. "We have help on the way."

"I don't need help," May objected, and this time her voice sounded a little stronger. She smiled up at Shafer and threw her arms around him, then looped her mother in on the hug as she said, "I just knew we were dead, Shafe. How did you…"

"Just a little swimming and stuff." He didn't have the energy to go into details. He just wanted to feel her breathing against him.

Mrs. Brimley tried to speak again but, much like Shafer at first, she found no words so she silently cried thankful tears.

Mr. Brimley seemed to be in shock as he processed everything that had happened. He took May by the hand. "I'm so glad you're okay, honey. Shafer, I don't know how to repay you. ...Again."

Shafer shook his head. "There's nothing to repay me for. We look out for those we care about, that's how it should be."

Mr. Brimley put his hand on Shafer's shoulder. "You're always going to be part of this family, Shafer."

"And I'm thankful for that," he answered with a smile, but then another thought struck him. "Actually, I know one way to thank me."

"What can I do, Shafer? Just say the word."

Shafer looked Mr. Brimley in the face and gave a weak smile. "Next time you get a new car, *you're* taking the first drive."

Mr. Brimley laughed and joined the family hug as two paramedics made their way down the hill.

SEVEN:
ALL ABOARD

As Shafer's suitcase was wheeled away on a cart, he asked May, "So when exactly do I get that back?"

"They'll use the tag to bring it to your room when we board," she explained. "I'm still shocked you've never taken a cruise before."

"My aunt gets seasick. But if this is good enough, then I might just have to tag along on all of yours."

"Oh, it's good," May promised. "At least, it's good if you like endless food, lots of activities, and hanging out on the beach."

"You coulda just stopped at endless food."

Mrs. Brimley pointed through an arched doorway. "We need to go in there so we can get boarded. *If* Stuart will ever get off the phone, that is."

Mr. Brimley mouthed *one second*, then said into his phone, "I know, Linus, and I'm not going to think about it for the next week, but when we get back I need answers, or we might be pushing out a lawsuit."

May rolled her eyes.

Mr. Brimley concluded, "Yes. Thank you so much. Please let Andrew know if you need anything. He's stepping in while I'm away. Thanks a lot." He ended the call.

As soon as he hung up, Mrs. Brimley asked, "What did they say?"

"They've scheduled a meeting with the manufacturer," Mr. Brimley replied. "And as soon as the car has been recovered and the diagnostics can be run, we will see what went wrong and how to move forward. The manufacturer says that it's simply impossible for it to have malfunctioned as it did, but we all know what happened."

May shook her head. "Dad, I'm fine and Shafer's fine, so I think we should just let it go. It was an accident, and luckily nobody was hurt. You heard the doctor. We didn't suffer any harm."

"I know, I know," Mr. Brimley said. "But there's nothing I care about in the world more than you, May, and their mistake put your life at risk. If it wasn't for Shafer and his quick thinking…" He didn't finish the sentence, but switched topics instead. "If we file a lawsuit, it's not about the money—it's about making sure that the manufacturer doesn't make a mistake like that again and take somebody else's life. It's a lesson."

"I agree with your father, May," Mrs. Brimley added, "And we know Shafer's family agrees, too. We're not trying to be mean, just make sure everybody is made more aware and nothing like that ever happens again."

"Fine." May crossed her arms. "But even more importantly, we're not gonna talk about it or think about it for a whole week, right? That's what you guys promised."

Mr. Brimley nodded. "From the moment our feet are onboard the ship, there will be no talk of lawsuits, business, or anything else that could rain on our vacation. We're going to have fun and enjoy some time off… that's a promise."

"And that sounds like a week of paradise," Shafer said. "Again, I'm so glad you guys invited me. Thank you."

Mrs. Brimley gave him a half-hug as they walked. "You're already part of the family, Shafer."

May slipped her fingers between his, and away they went.

So far, everything about the day had felt like an all-new adventure, especially the astonishment he'd felt when he'd first laid his eyes on their vessel, which was named the *Delta Voyager*.

Boarding the ship was a new experience, too. After handing over their bags to crew members, they passed through security, showed their boarding passes and passports to at least four or five different people, then entered a long building full of passengers: young couples standing too close to each other, chattering children, first-time cruisers and seasoned veterans.

That's how they'd ended up here, shuffling forward with the rest of the crowd. Nearby, an old man in a bucket hat, a floral shirt, and sunglasses snapped a picture of the boarding sign. Shafer pointed at the man and whispered to May, "Do you think he even realizes we haven't left yet?"

"Don't judge him too hard. I packed that same outfit in my bag," she teased.

Shafer and the Brimley's made their way through the building. Mr. Brimley pointed at some escalators and explained to Shafer, "Once we get up there, we'll walk up the tunnel to the boarding ramp, and then we can get on the ship from there."

Shafer glanced at his watch. "Already? Isn't it a little early?"

"Our rooms won't be ready yet, but we can go to the lido deck and get some food."

"The what?"

Mr. Brimley laughed. "You'll see."

They finally reached the escalator, and at the top of it, a Hispanic man with a camera stopped them. "Photos!" he called out. "Let me take your picture, *amigos*?"

Mr. Brimley nodded, so they were pulled in front of a backdrop that read *All Aboard the Delta Voyager!* After plastering on smiles, there was a flash, and the photographer offered a smile of his own as he reviewed the picture.

"This looks great, except..." He leaned in and studied the picture more intently. "Young man, your hat shadowed your face. Would you mind lifting it or taking it off?"

"Oh, yeah." Shafer pulled off his hat for another picture, but before the second flash ever came, he heard a shout.

A young girl, probably thirteen or so, pointed at him. "You're Shafer McCartney!"

Shafer continued looking at the photographer until the camera flashed once again, then turned to the girl and quickly pulled his hat back on over his head, even lower than it was before.

"Yeah, I am. What's your name?"

"I'm CeeJay, and, *ohmygosh* I can't believe it's really

you." She looked up at her parents. "That's Shafer! The boy who saved the world!"

"I don't really know about—"

"Can I take a picture with you?" she interrupted. "Please? Just one?"

Shafer sighed. "Yeah, I don't see what it could hurt." He moved away from the actual photo backdrop so the cruise portraits could resume, then let the girl's parents take a picture of them standing beside each other. He gave an awkward thumbs-up. The girl looked like she was going to melt.

Once the picture was taken, she asked, "Wait, if you're here, does that mean... are you... like, going on the cruise?"

Almost reluctantly, he nodded. "Yeah, with my girlfriend and her family."

"No way. There's, like, a real-life celebrity cruising with me!" She sounded like she couldn't believe the words as they spilled out of her mouth.

Shafer shook his head. "Not this week," he insisted. "I'm leaving all that behind and I'm gonna have a normal, fun vacation. But it was nice to meet you, CeeJay. Enjoy the cruise!"

"Yes! Maybe I'll see you around!" With that, her and her parents disappeared into the crowd.

May had a coy smile on her face. "Oh, Shafer, quite the growing following of fangirls you have."

Shafer chuckled. "Listen, too many more encounters like that this week and I'll be jumping overboard."

May laughed. "Don't worry. It's gonna be okay. I guess you can just wear that dorky hat everywhere we go."

Shafer took off his Washington Wizards hat for just a moment, looking at it before putting it back on his head. "Listen, I brought a second hat just in case you wanted to complain about this one."

"Whoa, two *different* hats. How lucky am I?"

Adopting a more serious tone, Shafer added, "I'm really excited. A week with you and your family is going to be great."

May took him by the hand once more. "I couldn't agree more. Now let's get on the boat!"

Once they did, Shafer found the "boat" to be more than even he could have ever expected. They entered at the middle of the ship, filtering in among more people, and he tried to take everything in, but there was too much to see: an enormous chandelier dangled overhead. A marble staircase spiraled up ahead of them. To both his left and right, glass elevators rose out of sight. He looked to one of them and saw a toddler with his face pressed to the glass, mesmerized by the lights, sights, and people.

"This is a boat… with *elevators*?" He pointed in near disbelief.

May bobbed her head. "I don't know about you, but I wouldn't want to take a dozen flights of stairs to get to the pool."

"There are twelve floors?"

"Twelve *decks*," she corrected. "But yeah, something like that. The ship's huge. This is the newest one with the cruise line, supposedly."

The crowds were loud enough that Mr. Brimley had to lean in to be heard. "Do you guys want to go grab a bite to eat while we wait?"

"Always," Shafer answered.

"Perfect. My kinda guy. Follow me."

They slipped into an elevator, joining an elderly couple as they rode to the tenth deck, which was labeled *lido*.

"What's a lido deck?" Shafer asked.

Mrs. Brimley explained, "It's where the buffet is, and there's the pool. There's probably a pizzeria, too. Usually, it's really casual."

Shafer nodded as he glanced out the elevator's glass wall behind him. They were near the top by now. From this high, all the passengers boarding the ship looked like little specks.

Mr. Brimley added, "The lido deck is probably my favorite hangout. You gotta see the cakes they serve, they're—"

Ding. The words were cut off as the elevator reached the top floor and slid open. Shafer filtered off first, and in doing so he caught his first glimpse of the lido deck. The first thing he noticed was a pool in the middle of the wide deck. Several bikini-clad girls were already swimming or laying out in lounge chairs despite the overcast sky.

He pointed to them, asking May, "How are they already in swimsuits and in the pool? It's been literally five minutes."

May shook her head. "It's time to show off while everybody's boarding, obviously."

Shafer fell in line and tried to catch up with Mr. Brimley, but he kept getting distracted by all the sights around him. From the pool to the hot tubs and the waterslide above them, it was a safe bet he'd spend a good deal of this vacation with pruned skin.

Then, something else caught Shafer's eye even more than the pools: the food. Suddenly mesmerized, he followed May's parents through a glass door, and that's when he laid his eyes on the buffet. As promised, it was tremendous: delicacies mixed with comfort food, a standalone salad bar, grillmasters working feverishly, and a whole wall of desserts.

"Look at this, May!" He didn't even give her a chance to respond. "Whoa! Look at those watermelons! They're… carved. Is that a lion?" His mind briefly flickered to Blasnoff's mansion.

May shook her head in bemusement. "You're such a dork. Go grab a plate so you can get something before our rooms are ready."

"I don't need a room," Shafer objected. "Just leave me at the buffet for a week."

"Excuse me, but who would I cuddle with during the open-water movie nights?"

Shafer looked around. "Maybe that guy in the Seahawks jersey? Sunglass tan lines over there. See him? Yeah, he'd be down."

"Shafer, he's like forty. I hate you sometimes, you know that?"

"I do." He put his arm around her. "But you can't love what you don't hate. Isn't that how it works?"

*****

The more Marco thought, the more briskly he walked.

To be fair, he was probably overthinking things. It wouldn't be the first time. But when you make a living by taking care of somebody else's property, it was always good to err on the side of caution.

For some reason, a thought kept nagging at him—a thought concerning the mishap with the car that had nearly killed May and Shafer. Mr. Brimley had a team of people investigating the accident, making sure there were no stones left unturned. If there was foul play at hand, then it would be discovered. Right?

Maybe Marco cared too much. Maybe he wasn't good at knowing his place. Or maybe, after twenty years, he felt like he was truly a part of the Brimley family, and therefore he wanted to help look after them.

For whatever reason, he couldn't help but wonder what if something underhanded had occurred. With all the worst-case scenarios tumbling through his mind, he walked to the gardens, looking for his new apprentice.

Marco found the man hard at work, as usual. This afternoon he was trimming the rose bushes that lined the pool.

"Sylvio?"

"Yes, sir?" Sylvio lowered his shears. "How can I help?"

Marco opened his mouth to speak, paused, then tried again. "I just needed to ask you something. About... well, about your first day here."

"Oh." A look of concern washed over Sylvio's face. "What's wrong? Did I make a mistake, sir?"

"I..." Marco trailed off as he looked at the new groundsman. From his smile to the ring of sweat on his shirt, he seemed like nothing but a hard-working man who was in a tight spot.

"What's wrong?"

Marco stammered. "I was just thinking about things, and..." Once again words escaped him. He immediately regretted coming.

"What's the problem?" Sylvio spoke softly. "Please, you can tell me. I'm new and learning—I won't be offended."

"It's not about the job. Well, not really." Marco tried to backtrack. "I was just thinking about what happened that day... with the new car."

"Oh." A flicker of recognition crossed Sylvio's face. "What about the car?"

Marco looked down. "It's probably nothing. I was just trying to figure out what could have gone wrong and—"

"They said it was some sort of system malfunction, right?"

"Yes."

"Then what's the issue, sir?"

At this point, Marco felt bad. He'd let a thought fester in his mind for too long, and now he was making something out of nothing. He didn't want to jeopardize his future working relationship with the new groundsman over something silly like this, but now he was in too deep.

"I just wanted to make sure that nothing happened between you and the car," Marco sheepishly admitted. "You don't seem like the kind of person to mess with somebody else's stuff, but if you accidentally messed something up looking at it or somethin', we should know."

"I see." The two words were Sylvio's only response.

"So did you mess with the car? I only ask because you were the only other person who could have been alone with it, and..."

Sylvio, with a much more solid voice, said, "If you're going to accuse me of something, sir, just say it."

"I'm not *accusing* you," Marco said, holding up his hands. "I just wanted to make sure that you didn't accidentally do this."

"Did you not check the cameras?" Sylvio asked.

"I thought about it because I really didn't want to say anything to you," Marco admitted. "But the car was in a blindspot."

Sylvio nodded. "I know."

Marco was confused. "Wait, you know?"

"Yes, and you're also standing in one right now." Cold certainly filled Sylvio's words. "And that's a good thing."

"What? Why is that a…"

Marco never finished his sentence.

Sylvio lunged forward with a blend of stealth and strength, impaling the garden shears in the man's chest.

The scream never escaped Marco's throat. He died immediately, dropping to the ground as his blood sprayed into the air.

Wiping off his safety glasses and looking down at Marco's body, Sylvio grimaced. This would require extensive clean-up, and he was already having a busy day. With a sigh, he wiped more blood off his hand before taking out his phone and dialing a number he'd memorized.

"Hello?" A gruff voice answered on the first ring. "Who's this?"

"Klaw."

"Klaw?" There was a laugh and change of tone. "What are you calling me for? I thought you were out of this life."

"One more job," Klaw replied. "That's it."

"And… what do you need me for?"

Klaw looked down at the body of the dead groundsman, a stunned expression plastered on his lifeless face. "I need you because… because I can't afford to be recognized."

"Isn't that how every job works?"

"Yes, but this is even more important than usual."

"How so?"

Klaw let out an annoyed huff. "My target has already seen me once, and despite my best efforts to orchestrate the perfect hit… Well, it went wrong."

"Wrong? How so?"

"I'm not telling you my life story over the phone. I'll explain in person."

"So what do you want from me?"

"Help." He said the word like it burned his tongue. "I need your help. I have a plan and I'll set everything up, but my cover is already nearly compromised, so you're my only option."

"What's in it for me?"

Klaw debated for just a moment, then reluctantly said, "Twenty-million. Don't bother asking for a penny more, though. The answer will be no."

"Hmm.…"

"What do you say?"

"When and where can we meet?"

EIGHT:
LIMELIGHT

There was a *click* as the automatic lock activated. The light on the scanner flashed green, and Shafer removed his room key and opened the door.

"Whoa…" Upon the first glimpse of his room, Shafer couldn't believe what he saw. It was big. It was comfortable. It was fancy, too. The opposite wall had a large window, and out of the window, he could see open water.

"Do you like it?" May asked him as she followed him inside.

"I… yes. Wow." He was drawn to the window which looked out at the water, and beyond that, the beach. "I thought cruise rooms were small. That's what I read online."

May nodded. "Some are. But this is a suite, technically. The one my family is staying in is the exact same."

"All this is… mine?"

She nodded again.

"And you guys are right next door?"

"Yeah, right there." She pointed to their left, then joined him by the window, looking out at the bustling Florida coast. "I'm ready to go."

"Go? Like... for the ship to roll out?"

"For the ship to *debark*," she corrected with a giggle. "But yes."

"You and your fancy ship words..." Shafer wrapped an arm around her, gazing out the window. "But why are you so anxious to leave?"

May leaned her head against him. "See those people out there on the beach?"

"Yeah."

"Every single one of those people knows who you are, Shafer," she said. "And every single one of those people would want to shake your hand and take a picture with you."

"I mean, maybe..."

"You've handled it so well—the transition from high schooler to international sensation—but I know it's not easy."

He didn't respond, only watched as people continued splashing around the beach.

"You're stressed. You always wear that stupid hat or sunglasses and hide from people. And you won't say no to anything, so you're just stuck taking care of everybody else and won't spend any time taking care of yourself."

"Are you accusing me of being... nice?"

May sighed, rubbing a hand on his back. "I'm accusing you of not focusing on what matters, of focusing on everybody else and not taking time for *Shafer*."

As he watched waves roll towards the crowds on the

beaches, Shafer realized something: May was right.

"I'll tell you what," he said, putting his other arm around her and turning to face her. "I'm going to change that. This week is my week. It's *our* week. It's about having fun and enjoying the activities and time with family and each other. So, from this point on, I won't take any more pictures with people, and I'm done being a 'celebrity' or whatever."

"Shafer..." May looked up into his eyes. "Do you mean it?"

"Absolutely."

Suddenly, a tapping came on the open door to the suite. A tall man with a grey beard was peeking his head in their room. He wore a white collared shirt, white pants, and a ridiculous-looking white hat. With one look, Shafer knew this man had to be the captain.

When he saw Shafer and May sharing a moment, he hurried to say, "I am sorry to interrupt! My sincerest apologies. I can come back..."

"No worries," Shafer objected with a laugh. "You're completely fine."

"Are you sure?"

"Absolutely."

Still looking embarrassed, the man walked into the room. "I was talking to Mr. Brimley and saw your door was open, and just..."

"It's totally fine," Shafer repeated, letting go of May and walking toward the door. "How are you?"

"Very fortunate," the man replied. He spoke with a raspy, friendly one. "I just found out this morning that we have a couple of VIPs sailing with us this week, and I wanted to come down and meet *the* Shafer McCartney

and the Brimley family before we set sail."
Shafer grinned and stuck his hand out to shake. "That's awesome. I'm stoked to be here. And I'm Shafer."
"I'm Charles Graf, captain of the *Delta Voyager*, and I will sail her at ease knowing that if something is going to go wrong, we have a real-life superhero on board."
"You're too kind," Shafer responded. "But I was just telling May that I'm done with all those shenanigans. This is going to be a week of relaxation and fun for me, just like everybody else on board."
Captain Graf gave a wheezy laugh. "So if something goes wrong on the boat, does that mean you *won't* be saving the day?"
"Let's just hope it doesn't come to that," Shafer said with a spirited shrug. "You don't usually have world-threatening emergencies aboard these ships, right?"
"No robots or bombs, no. At least not usually."
"Good. I've had all that I can take of those for a while." Shafer gestured to May. "This is May."
May flashed her dazzling smile and said something to Graf, but Shafer didn't hear. He'd tuned out for a moment, lost in her smile.
When he rejoined the conversation, Graf asked, "So how long have you been together?"
May looked at Shafer. "Like… a month? A bit more. We met at Blasnoff's and just really clicked."
Shafer nodded. "She's right. I met her by accidentally bumping her with a door, and that was probably the greatest thing I've done in my life."
"That's quite a big statement coming from somebody who goes on spy missions and saves the world," Graf chuckled. "I should go soon because we need to set

sail, but before I do, I have something to ask."

"Anything," Shafer answered. "What's up?"

"Tonight, as you know, is the Captain's Dinner in the *Seven Seas Restaurant,"* Graf said. "Everybody will be coming together for a big meal, and it's a lot of fun. Shafer, I was wanting to know if you'd be willing to participate in a toast. I'd call you up, let you say a few words, and then we'd have a toast to you and your heroics. A free drink to all of the adults. Are you…"

"Not old enough," Shafer laughed. "And I really, really appreciate the offer." He glanced at May. "But I'm going to have to pass. I've made a commitment to both myself and May that I'll focus on being a normal teenager and having fun this week, so a toast would probably get that off on the wrong foot."

"I completely understand that," Graf said with a nod. "Not only do I understand, but I'm very impressed. You're quite the young man, Shafer. You have everything figured out, it seems."

"Definitely not, but I'm working on it."

Graf took a card from his shirt pocket and handed it to Shafer. "Here's my number for you and May. I'm not sure if your cell phones will have any signal on the open water, but you can call on your room phone or cell at any time if you need *anything.*"

"Wow, thank you."

"And thank *you,*" Graf answered. "I'll leave you guys to it. I hope it's a great cruise." With that, he slipped out of the room.

The ship hadn't even debarked yet, and Shafer was feeling the magic of the open water. His stomach fluttered with excitement between being there with May and the view of the ocean outside his large window.

In only seconds, another knock came at the door and Mr. Brimley entered.

May turned to Shafer. "I'm going to unpack, and you should too. Then there's the safety meeting."

"Safety meeting? Where's that?"

"Um, it's gotta be around here somewhere. They usually announce it about fifteen times, so no worries. It won't take long, either. There's not much to say, anyway. We're as safe as can be."

*****

"So you're telling me that your elaborate hit on a tech billionaire was foiled by... a fourteen-year-old boy?"

"He's sixteen, I think."

"Oh, my mistake. In that case, it's totally understandable." The answer dripped with sarcasm.

Klaw leaned back in his chair, staring up at the ceiling. "I see your point."

"You're losing a step, old man. Father time is catching up to you."

Keeping a level expression, Klaw looked across the table at the man half-reading over a report. This was Ash. He had dark blond hair, a muscular build, and bright blue eyes. In this industry, people didn't make friends, but Ash was the closest thing to one that Klaw had.

"I'm not losing a step. I'm just... becoming wiser."

"Wise enough to get beaten by a child." Ash took a cigarette from his jacket and lit it. "You seem to be overlooking that."

"I didn't get 'beaten by a child'," Klaw argued. "The

universe screwed me over. Fate. Something. I had all the pieces in place, and that car *should* have killed Brimley, but instead, that rich bastard let his daughter's boyfriend take the first ride. Unbelievable."

Ash ran his eyes over the report. "I would've given my right arm to drive a car like that at his age."

"Not for the kind of ride that boy took, I assure you."

"He seems to have come out of it fine."

"Just luck."

Ash finally looked up, holding Klaw's gaze. "I know what boy we're talking about. I know *exactly* who he is."

Klaw was suddenly on edge, growing even more defensive. "What do you mean?"

"We're talking about the international sensation. The boy who exposed Blasnoff and saved the world. The boy that every damn girl in America can't get enough of, including my daughter."

"You have a—"

"Shafer McCartney," Ash interrupted. "That's the boy, right?"

Slowly, Klaw nodded. "That's the one."

For the first time, Ash brought the cigarette to his lips. He took a long draw before blowing a puff of smoke into the air. "So you truly think the boy who's accomplished so much and *then* survived the car ride is... lucky?"

"Yes."

"Then you're a fool. He's not lucky, he's *talented*," Ash insisted. "Incredibly talented. Crafty and quick-thinking, or—"

"We're digressing," Klaw said. "This isn't about the boy. It's about Brimley, and that's why I need your help.

The boy doesn't matter at all."

"He *does* matter." Another puff of smoke. "He matters because, according to you, he's joining the Brimley's on the cruise, so we've got to consider that. We need to think of him as an extra level of protection for Brimley."

"He's a child!"

"I'd agree with you if he had gotten lucky once," Ash said. "Maybe even twice. But *three* times? *Four*? There's something to the McCartney boy, and we need to anticipate him getting involved in whatever you have planned."

"I already have," Klaw said, leaning forward. "So let's just stop talking about the boy and get back to briefing. Are you ready to move on?"

Ash looked at the paper in front of him, back up to Klaw, and then he smirked.

"What? What's so funny?" Klaw suddenly sounded defensive despite his best efforts to keep the snappiness out of his tone.

Ash smirked. "Relax. I'm just ruffling your feathers. The boy has some talent for sure, but I'm not worried about him. I can just tell he's gotten under your skin, and frankly, that's kinda funny. I couldn't help myself."

Annoyed with himself, Klaw sat back in his chair and ran a hand through his hair, trying to play it off. "I'm fine. I'm not thinking about Shafer. I'm thinking about Brimley, and I have everything planned perfectly."

"So... what do you want me to do?"

Klaw took another paper from inside his jacket, unfolded it, and slid it to Ash. "The family is currently on a cruise heading toward the Caribbean, and soon you will be, too."

Ash raised an eyebrow. "I'm getting a vacation out

of this?"

"You're getting a new identity and occupation," Klaw corrected as he took out two cards and slid those to Ash as well. "Here's your driver's license, and here's your passport."

"What will I be doing with these, pray tell?"

"You'll be captaining a cruise ship."

Concern flickered across Ash's face. "I appreciate you recognizing my intelligence and the breadth of my work, but you do realize I know nothing about sailing, right?"

"That's why you're going to be a captain-in-training," Klaw corrected. "At least for your time aboard the ship. I have it all set up with both parties."

Ash looked over the driver's license. "Ben Szalay. Great name."

"I agree, *Ben*. You will be boarding the *Delta Voyager* at Grand Turk. The captain has been informed you'll be shadowing him for the cruise, and while you're on board, you'll find out where Brimley is staying, and then you are to perform the hit—the details are outlined below."

"I think we need to renegotiate the price," Ash said with an arched eyebrow. "I'm not sure what you're getting paid for this, but it sounds like I'm going to be doing all the work."

"I've done all the set-up," Klaw objected. "I came up with the plan, and I've even come up with the backup plan… just in case. See the bottom of the page?"

Ash's eyes scanned down, and after a moment, he whistled. "Damn. You're willing to resort to that?"

"If I have to," Klaw said.

"You'd kill… everybody." Ash's voice was filled with

a strange mixture of objection and admiration.

"I was told it has to look like an accident, and that was at the forefront of all decision-making, from the car to this."

Ash lazily held the cigarette between two fingers, looking across the table. "You said you killed the gardener... What becomes of that?"

"That identity—Sylvio—is long gone," Klaw said. "No worries about that. Our only concern is what's next, what I need you to do. So what do you say? You have the plans, just make the call."

Ash put the cigarette to his lips for another drag as he leaned in to look at the report Klaw had given him. There was the silence of contemplation, then he finally said, "If I were talking to anybody else in the world right now, I'd say no."

"But...?"

"But I've learned two things in life, Klaw. I've learned not to cross my wife and I've learned not to doubt you or your plans. I've seen you take on some pretty impossible things... and I've never seen you fail. Not once."

Klaw couldn't fight the hint of a smile from spreading across his face. "So you're in?"

"I'm in."

Klaw stood. "Good. Memorize those plans. Memorize the paper. Memorize your new identity. Then, when you're finished, burn it all. Leave nothing to chance. Wait at least seventy-five minutes to leave this room, and contact me when you are ready for phase two. You know how to get ahold of me."

Ash took the cigarette lighter from his jacket pocket and set one of the pages on fire as Klaw watched. "Wow, anything *else?*"

The question was sarcastic, but Klaw answered nonetheless. "Yes, actually."

"What would that be?"

"The boy we were talking about earlier, Shafer."

"Yeah?" Ash's eyes dropped to the smoldering remains of the paper on the table. "What about him?"

"This is very important: Do not touch him. He is not to be harmed in any way, understood?"

"Um, yeah... but why? What if you default to plan B?"

Klaw said, "We will figure out something. But you can't kill him. Got it?"

"Yeah... sure." Ash sounded skeptical, but Klaw didn't care.

Klaw added, "Don't screw this up. This is retirement for me and a pretty penny for you."

"I've never let you down," Ash said matter-of-factly. "Trust me, I've got this under control. Stuart Brimley is never getting off that ship."

NINE:
IF YOU LIKE PIÑA COLADAS

"Okay, can we never get off this ship?" It was the first thing Shafer could say as he set down his breakfast plate, which was covered by an omelet so large that it draped off both sides.

"You don't have to get off, I guess," May replied. "But you'd miss out on Grand Turk this afternoon. I've heard it has the prettiest water of any of the stops."

Shafer lifted his omelet to uncover a steaming side of hash browns. "Clear water is still just water, right?"

"Well, I'll also be wearing that new swimsuit I showed you."

"I guess the buffets can wait."

May laughed.

"How's breakfast?" Mrs. Brimley asked as she approached the table armed with a plate of fruit and a glass of orange juice.

"I haven't tried it yet because I need a roadmap just to figure out where to dig in," Shafer quipped as he rotated his plate a bit. "But my omelet has thirteen ingredients and weighs as much as a small dog, so I'm thinking breakfast is off to a good start." He tried a bite, then nodded his approval.

Mr. Brimley swooped in behind Mrs. Brimley, carrying two plates of food and a carefully balanced cup of coffee. He looked at his wife's plate and asked, "With everything on the buffet, you got eight pieces of fruit?"

"We're here for a week," she responded immediately. "I'm not going to kill myself on the first morning."

"Touché. I'll probably be sick by the end of the week." Mr. Brimley pulled up his chair. He took a sip of coffee. "So, Shafer, you've got your first day of cruising under your belt. Or half a day, at least. Whatcha think?"

Shafer swallowed a bite of omelet and used his fork to fight back a loose strand of cheese dangling from his lip. "I think someday I'm going to retire and move aboard a cruise ship. You think they'd make me get off the boat if I book back-to-back cruises for months at a time?"

Mrs. Brimley laughed.

Mr. Brimley said, "I like the way you think. I'm sure you could work something out with the cruise line."

More seriously, Shafer added, "I'm surprised how smooth it is. Most of the time I can't even tell I'm on a boat."

"Yeah." Mr. Brimley sliced a link of sausage. "I've been on probably a dozen cruises over the years and only experienced rough seas a handful of times. When it does happen it can be brutal, but it's pretty unlikely."

Shafer took another bite. "I'm also surprised there's like... so much to do. The sail-away party and dinner were great last night, but the party doesn't stop. *Ever.* May showed me the activities schedule. There's just so much. I want to do everything I can."

"I thought you never wanted to leave the buffet?" May pointed out jokingly.

"Technically, I said I never wanted to leave the *ship*. That way the food would always be like two minutes away. And speaking of endless buffets, do you guys know where the gym is?"

Mr. Brimley sighed. "I miss the days when I had that kind of energy."

"You could join Shafer," Mrs. Brimley suggested. "I'm sure he wouldn't mind."

"Not at all," Shafer encouraged. "I usually try to go early in the mornings, but I'll go whenever you want."

Mr. Brimley shook his head. "I appreciate the offer, but go ahead. I like my sleep and food way too much. I'll get back with it when we get home."

"Yeah, you use our home gym *so* much," May teased. "I'll go with you, Shafer. How early are you thinking?"

"I don't know. Like six?"

"Six? Forget that. I was thinking like nine-thirty."

He laughed. "I'm a morning person. You know that."

May shook her head.

Mrs. Brimley asked, "Have you ever been to any islands before, Shafer?"

"Um, I'm not sure if Australia counts," he responded. "We went on a vacation to Sydney last year. But as far as tropical islands go, no. We try to take a vacation most summers, but it's usually either a foreign city or a cabin in the woods—my uncle really likes that kind of thing."

"Grand Turk is going to be a new experience for you, I think. We've booked an excursion that's a private beach with cabanas and some sort of local lunch."

"Have you been there before?"

"It's been a long time, but yes. May, you were only like five or six."

May shook her head. "I don't remember."

"It's the prettiest beach I've ever seen in my life," Mr. Brimley said after taking another sip of coffee. "If you're into beaches, it's one you have to see to see, I can tell you that."

"Then I trust you guys on this," Shafer replied, forking a bite of hash browns. "I can't wait."

*****

Mr. Brimley was right.

The beach was everything Shafer expected, and then some. It was a postcard-ready sight, with white sand and crystal-clear water that seemed too perfect to actually be real. It was the sort of thing that should only appear in movies, the too-good-to-be-true natural beauty of the world that was as removed from human tainting as possible.

As magical as the scenery was, however, not everything had gone perfectly.

There'd been a... mishap.

It started when he'd decided to go for a swim in the ocean, using a snorkeling kit that had been provided. The water was as clear as advertised: no matter how far out he ventured, he could see the bottom of the ocean: the sand, the fish, the plants, the algae, and even fields of beautiful coral.

At one point, he'd spotted a shell. It was there, fifteen feet below the surface of the water, glimmering white against the seagrass around it. Curiosity led him to dive down toward it, but when he reached out and scooped up the shell in his hand, something happened.

A feeling. It washed over him, more pressing and restricting than all the water around him, swallowing him up and pushing down on him.

Suffocating him.

The feeling stemmed from a memory, one that was recent enough to send his heart racing. As he floated against the seafloor, looking at the shell in his hand through the goggles on his face, claustrophobia clawed at his chest.

Only days before, he'd been in this sort of situation: stuck at the bottom of the ocean and clutching onto something while the surface, oxygen, and *life* hovered somewhere distant above his head, somewhere too far away for it to do him any good.

And as those thoughts rolled through his mind, his body froze. He couldn't move. He couldn't force the feeling out of his head.

What if he hadn't been so lucky during the car crash? One wrong move—just a wasted second or two—and his life would be much different. Instead of vacationing with May, he might be attending her funeral. He might be drowning in the guilt of not being good enough, of not being fast enough, of not being strong enough.

He might have lost her.

Or, even worse, they both could have died.

He could have drowned, too.

But he hadn't. He'd survived, May'd survived, and somehow, he'd come out of it alive. Somehow… he always did.

At least, at this point, he always *had*.

And as quick as it came, the feeling resided. Clamping his hands around the shell, Shafer kicked off the sand below, and soon he was breaking through the surface. The air was sweet as he breathed it in deeply before swimming back to shore.

May was waiting for him on the sand. "You were under for a while Shafe! I was getting worried."

He smiled, pulled off his swim mask, and pretended everything was all right. "Close your eyes."

"What?"

"You heard me. Close 'em."

"Okay…" She closed her eyes. "Now what?"

"Hold out your hand."

She did, and he delicately placed the shell in her palm. "I want you to have this. It… it reminded me of you."

She opened her eyes and immediately smiled as she identified her present. "Aw, Shafer, it's beautiful."

"And that's why it reminded me of you," he told her. What he failed to add, however, was the darker thought going through his mind: as beautiful as the shell was, it was thin. It was delicate. It wouldn't take much to break it, for it to be gone forever, and that's how May was, too. That's how *everybody* was, and he was just now starting to see it.

"Let's go to the cabana. My dad said they're serving virgin piña coladas."

"What now?"

"There's no alcohol in them."

"Gotcha."

"Would you drink one?"

"Oh yeah." He nodded. "You know what they say: hydration is key."

"Have you said that before? Sounds familiar."

"I mean… maybe?"

They headed back to the cabana, the sand soft and damp underfoot. It squished between Shafer's toes, and he turned back to see his footprints leading away from the water.

"After we get a drink, will you go swimming with me?" May asked. "I had to change while you were out there."

He looked at her, taking in the billowing white material wrapped from her torso to her knees. "Yeah, I noticed. Is that, like… a toga?"

"No! It's a *coverup*. C'mon. They're cute and fashionable."

"Um… maybe if you're a monk."

"Hey, take that back. Shafer…"

"Seriously, I thought you brought a Snuggie… but without the sleeves."

May kicked sand at him, pelting his calves with the tiny particles. "Don't act like you're the pinnacle of fashion either with those swim trunks. Are they…"

Shafer looked down to his black swimsuit that was covered in white writing. "They're mathematical equations."

"Seriously? Why do you have a swimsuit covered in algebra?"

"Most of this is calculus, I think," he corrected. Noticing the look she gave him, he asked, "What? Numbers are cool."

"I don't believe this. You're a *nerd*."

"Me? No."

"Definitely a nerd. This will be revisited later." She walked into the cabana, Shafer following closely behind.

Mr. Brimley was inside, reading a book with a drink in his hand. The drink, however, wasn't in a glass, but rather a hollowed-out coconut.

"Hey, guys!" He looked up from the book. "How was the water, Shafer?"

"It's great. Super clear."

"You're right about that." Mr. Brimley reached for a tray beside him, then extended it out to Shafer and May. "Do you like piña coladas?"

On the tray were two more coconut drinks, just like Mr. Brimley's, and both Shafer and May took one. After the first sip through the bright orange straw, Shafer said, "This is awesome."

"Nothing like a fresh piña colada," Mr. Brimley agreed. "What do you guys have planned?"

"We're going swimming in a bit," May said. "And I'm gonna lay out for a while."

"Yeah, that sounds good to me, too," Shafer agreed.

"That's what Heather went to do." Mr. Brimley pointed behind him, through the wall. "She'll be asleep in no time, I promise."

"Not a bad way to spend a day."

The three of them made small talk in the cabana, enjoying their drinks and the tropical breeze as the waves gently crashed to the shore. Mr. Brimley was the kind of person who knew a little bit about everything, and Shafer enjoyed the talk so much that he almost didn't want to leave when May asked him if he was ready to swim. Nevertheless, he agreed. "Yeah, let's do it."

They walked back out on the beach, and as they headed to the water, May shrugged off her swim-wrap.

Shafer tried not to stare, but he didn't succeed.

May was stunning, wearing a black-and-white bikini that fit *too* perfectly, and she wasn't afraid to let him know she could feel his gaze. She looked back over her shoulder and said, "You have all this tropical scenery to take in, and you're staring at my butt?"

"Me? No..." Flushed with embarrassment, he mumbled, "I was looking at the ocean. I've heard you can find crabs at the edge of the water."

May raised an eyebrow. "Is that the story you're going with?"

"Just get in the water."

"Not yet." She held up her phone. "We gotta take a cute beach selfie first. Get in here."

The "cute beach selfie" ended up being seventeen less-fortunate pictures that didn't make the cut, followed by one picture she finally deemed worthy.

As May thumbed through them, she cooed, "Look at how cute we look in this one."

Shafer peered over her shoulder. "What's the difference between that one and the twelve before it?"

"My smile's better in this one. And the lighting, I think. I just look so happy."

Shafer gently reached around her and turned off her phone.

"Hey, what was that for?" May asked indignantly.

He pointed toward the ocean. "Listen to yourself.

DELTA ADRIFT

We're on a tropical beach. We're drinking from coconuts and spending time with each other. We're away from the real world and all its problems. Stop trying to *look* happy and just *be* happy. Let's just enjoy each other. Who cares what that looks like to anybody else?"

She set her phone down on her towel and met his gaze. "You know, you're occasionally kinda sweet."

"You don't say."

"I mean it. You're full of surprises, and I like it."

"Good, because I have one more surprise for you."

"What do you…"

He didn't give her time to finish before he scooped her up and ran into the ocean. She giggled and screamed the whole way as he carried her into the water, and soon they were deep enough that she could no longer stand, so she grabbed onto his shoulders.

Together, they swam, but this time, there were no mishaps. Nothing clicked inside Shafer's head or shut off his brain. Maybe it was because he didn't venture as far from the shore. Maybe because he didn't dive down. Or maybe it was something else: the fact that he had May by his side as proof that she was okay, that he had saved her, and that he was still surrounded by those he cared about.

For whatever reason, Shafer had fun. He splashed, laughed, floated, and talked to May. They didn't talk about anything in particular, either, just anything that drifted into the conversation as they drifted through the water.

They were in the ocean for much longer than he ever expected, but he didn't want to go. If he could have frozen time then and there, he would have done it.

But eventually, the waves picked up, the saltwater began pruning his body, and it was time to get out. With

May's hand in his own, they walked back from the beach, leaving two sets of footprints side-by-side.

"That was so nice, Shafe," she said. "I can't tell you how long it's been since it was just the two of us and we were able to talk."

"I know," he agreed. "But tread lightly. Last time you said that we almost died in a car crash."

"Thank goodness there are no cars here." She picked up her swim wrap, but only carried it.

"You can say that again."

May pointed to the cabana., "I brought a blanket in my beach bag. I'll grab it, and then we can spread it out over there."

He followed her finger. "That sounds good. I need a towel."

"Let the sun dry you. It's better that way."

She was correct. In no time, the two of them were sprawled out on a blanket beside each other, face-down. The sun beat down on Shafer's back, and its heat pulled the water from his swimsuit.

This is the life, he decided. The only people after his attention were people he cared about. The only person asking to take pictures with him was his girlfriend. And the ambient rumble of traffic and crowds had been replaced by the tranquil wash of the waves to the shore.

This truly *was* paradise, and with the sun beating down on him, coaxing him to relax, Shafer had no worries in the world, just happiness in his heart. With that, he closed his eyes.

When he opened them again, something had changed.

Something was wrong.

May was still asleep beside him, but that was about the only thing that hadn't changed. The sun was no longer bright. Instead, the sky was overcast. Shafer felt two drops of rain pelt his back, right between his shoulder blades, and the sea breeze had turned into aggressive gusts of wind, so much so that the waves were rolling close to their blanket.

Mr. Brimley was outside of the cabana, talking to Mrs. Brimley, and when he saw Shafer standing, he said, "Shafer, great timing. I was about to wake you two."

"Is everything okay?" Shafer shook some sand from his hair.

"Mostly," Mr. Brimley said. "I just talked to the locals, and there's a storm brewing. A pretty ominous one, apparently. I was hoping it might be just a tropical shower, but I think our beach day is going to be cut a bit short."

"Oh... that's no good."

"Nothing too serious, but enough that it would probably be a good idea to head back to the ship. Can you wake May?"

Shafer kneeled down and put his hand on May's back. Her skin was soft under his. "May?" He gently shook her.

"Huh?" She raised her head. "What's wrong, Shafe?"

"There's a storm coming. We're gonna head back to the ship."

"Oh, okay." She still sounded groggy. "Can you hand me my wrap?"

"Sorry about this, guys," Mr. Brimley apologized. "I guess we just have really bad timing."

"No, don't worry about it at all." Shafer waved his hand dismissively. "Not your fault, and we still had a great time here. Right, May?"

"Yeah." She still only sounded half-awake.

"Good," Mr. Brimley answered. "Heather and I did too." He peeked back in the cabana, then said, "I think I've got everything, so let's head back and beat the storm. If we leave now, I bet we can still eat lunch on the ship."

"Is it gonna be bad? The storm, I mean." Finally, May sounded a little more coherent.

"No," Mr. Brimley shook his head. "The locals aren't too concerned, so it's probably nothing to worry about. Just some showers, I'm sure. Nothing to worry about at all."

TEN: GETTING CAUGHT IN THE RAIN

Mr. Brimley wasn't the only one who'd had the idea of boarding the *Delta Voyager*. By the time their group had made it back to the dock past the various shops and tourist-grabbing sales of Grand Turk, the boarding line was fifty people deep. Behind them, even more swimsuit-clad people were shuffling into line.

And the line wasn't the only thing growing. The intensity of the storm was, too. What had started as light raindrops had quickly grown in size, and soon they were pelting down on everybody in line. This was nothing like the rain Shafer was used to. Today it seemed as if the air had turned into water faster than he could snap his fingers.

Mr. Brimley wiped his brow. "I guess we should've brought an umbrella."

"I never made it to the ocean, so I guess the ocean was brought to me," Mrs. Brimley chimed in. Her words were barely audible over the rain pelting the boarding ramp.

May's swim wrap was soaked and matted to her skin. She tried to adjust it, but it didn't move.

Over the rain slamming into the boarding deck, Shafer quipped, "Your toga isn't waterproof?"

She rolled her eyes. "No, but at least it's not covered in slope-intercept form."

"Wow, now *you're* the nerd."

Boom. A rumble of thunder shook Shafer's chest. The clouds overhead were ominous, and the ocean had changed, too. No longer was it clear and bright; now it was dark and choppy. Waves were slapping near the top of the pier, reaching out and grabbing at the tourists.

In the violent waters, the *Delta Voyager* was responding as expected, rocking side-to-side as the ocean swelled around it.

May pointed at the ship as another clap of thunder shook the sky. "Do you really think we should board the ship? Is it gonna be safe?"

Mr. Brimley was unconcerned. "Yeah, it might have a little sway to it, but these boats are built to withstand a lot more than a storm like this. It gets a lot worse in the deep waters."

May looked skeptical.

"Would you rather stay here?" He offered. "We can wait for it to blow over some."

Squinting through the downpour at the growing line of people behind her, May shook her head. "Nah, we've stood here for long enough that I don't want to go back.

Plus, I'm kinda hungry."

Shafer silently agreed. His stomach was already growling. Fortunately, the wait in the rain didn't take too much longer, and soon he was following the sopping-wet Brimley family through the security check.

As May placed her new phone in a tray on the conveyor belt to bypass the security scan, she grumbled, "I just hope it still works. I don't want to go through two phones in a week."

"See, that's the advantage of never actually having your phone with you," Shafer replied as water ran from his hair onto his face. He wanted to towel it off, but his towel was soaked, too.

"Yeah, I can't think of one single time that you might have needed your phone but didn't have it," May shot back.

"Okay, touché. You got me there."

"Also, what if you wanted pictures?"

He couldn't help but grin. "Why would I need to take any pictures when my girlfriend is May Brimley, the *queen* of social media?"

"Good point. I've got the eye for it."

Once they'd cleared security, Mrs. Brimley led them through the maze of a hallway to the elevator. As they walked, Shafer felt the floor pitch under his feet. It was disorienting, like his feet weren't treading on solid ground, although his brain was telling him a different story.

"You don't get seasick, d'ya Shafer?" Mr. Brimley asked.

"I... um, I don't think so. I guess it's always good to find out."

The lobby in front of the elevators was full of people. Mrs. Brimley said, "Looks like we'll be waiting for a bit."

Shafer temporarily checked out of the conversation when he noticed something that didn't make sense. *Someone* that didn't make sense. Standing across the hall, dressed from head to toe in white, was the ship's captain.

Except it wasn't.

This man wasn't Captain Graf. He wasn't old enough. He was taller, more muscular. He was built like an NFL linebacker and looked like he'd been through a war, like he'd seen far too much in a lifetime for a man in his mid-thirties.

He noticed Shafer's gaze, and even though Shafer debated trying to play it off, he'd been caught staring too intently, so he nodded a greeting.

The man walked over to him. He began to say something but then paused, leaned forward, and whispered, "Are you… are you Shafer McCartney?"

"Yeah," Shafer answered, extending his hand, only for it to be swallowed in the enormous paw of the man in white. "And you're… not Captain Graf."

The man let out a laugh. "You noticed a difference? I thought I was his spitting image." He shook Shafer's hand. "Ben Szalay, captain-in-training."

By now, the Brimley family had come over, too. Mr. Brimley shook hands with Szaley, asking, "Did I hear captain-in-training?"

Szalay nodded. "Yes sir. It's an eight-month program in which I shadow some of the best captains of the cruise line. Captain Graf is one of them, if not *the* best, so I'm starting with him. I'm Captain Szalay, but you can call me Ben."

"Stuart. Stuart Brimley."

A look of recognition flashed in Szalay's eyes. "You don't say. Nice to meet you, sir. I worked in the accounting sector when I was younger and we used one of the first iterations of Razor. I can't tell you how much easier it was to do the calculations we'd been doing by hand."

"A long-time Edge customer," Mr. Brimley approved. "Always a pleasure. I'm glad you liked the program. It's come a long way since then."

As Shafer listened to them talk, he was reminded that he wasn't entirely sure what Mr. Brimley's Razor program even did so he made a mental note to ask about it later.

"Here's an elevator, dear," Mrs. Brimley said as she put a hand on Mr. Brimley's back.

"I'll join you," Szalay said. "*If* you don't mind."

"Not at all. Please, tag along."

Together the Brimley's, Shafer, and Szalay boarded the elevator. Mr. Brimley punched the button for the ninth floor, which started glowing, and the doors closed. "Where are you heading, Ben?"

"Floor ten. And you're headed to nine? Is that the suites?"

Mr. Brimley nodded. "Yessir."

"The ones at the very front of the ship? The view is incredible from those."

"Yessir. Suite 9-B. It's really nice."

As the elevator began to rise, the ship pitched again.

Shafer leaned with his back against the wall of the elevator, shaking his head. "Geez," he mumbled.

A smile cracked Szalay's serious expression. "My friend, if you think you can feel it down here, wait until you get to the upper decks."

"Sounds like lunch is going to be an adventure. I can't wait."

He did wait, though. Before heading to the lido deck, they stopped at their rooms. Shafer quickly dried off and changed before meeting Mr. and Mrs. Brimley in the hallway. May took what seemed like forever, all while Mr. Brimley complained about how long it takes teenage girls to perform simple tasks, but eventually, they all headed to the lunch spread.

As Szalay had predicted, the upper levels of the boat were rocking aggressively, even to the point that Shafer had to grab onto the handrails as he led the way down the stairs.

"Are you sure you're okay with this, Shafer?" Mr. Brimley asked. "I didn't think it would be *this* bad. I don't want you eating lunch if you're feeling queasy. We can go find a place on land."

"We're changed and dry. No worries," Shafer insisted. "I don't feel sick, thankfully. I'm just trying to adjust. Find my sea legs, or whatever. If I'm walking like I had too many piña coladas, just know that I'm too young to drink."

"I never thought I'd be so happy about a boy wanting to date my daughter," Mr. Brimley said with a grin.

Shafer staggered down the stairs, finally reaching the lido deck. It was, as expected, empty. The pool in the middle had overflowed, and water sloshed across the entire deck. Together they waded across the deck, finally reaching the buffet with squidgy steps.

As a particularly violent pitch of the boat sent Mr. Brimley shuffling toward the wall, he said, "Well, this probably means more food for us, I guess?"

Despite the rocking of the boat, navigating the buffet went well for the most part. Shafer filled a plate with food and was about to sit down, but changed his mind. "I think I'm going to go to the bathroom first," he told May and Mrs. Brimley. "Do you know…"

May pointed. "Right out there."

"Thanks."

After washing his hands and leaving the fancy restroom, he heard something.

Something that stopped him in his tracks.

He leaned his head to the side, listening intently as the rain pounded the deck above his head. Had he truly heard something, or was he just imagining it?

There was a moment of silence—apart from the rain, at least—and he was beginning to think his mind was playing tricks on him. But then, as he was about to join the Brimley's, he heard it again.

One word, faint and weak, but still a shout: "Help!"

"Ah, crap," Shafer muttered. Glancing back into the cafeteria, he debated running back and grabbing the Brimley's, but the urgency behind the cry for help made him rethink. What if he didn't have time?

With a nervous sigh, he ran out of the cafeteria and into the storm. As soon as he passed from under the awning, the rain pelted him. It was crashing down on the deck so hard that the initial rush of water swirling around his feet nearly swept him off balance.

Shafer squinted as the rain and splatter slapped him in the face. Cupping his hands in front of his mouth, he yelled, "Hello?"

No response.

Then, almost as faintly as he'd heard it the first time,

he heard it again: "Help!"

This time, Shafer had a heading: the cry was coming from above him. He grabbed the railing of the stairs and began to ascend as water cascaded down them like a waterfall.

"I'm coming!" Grabbing the handrails, he fought his way up the stairs, but the boat rocked again and he stumbled, slamming his knee into the stairs and swearing.

"Over here!" The call sounded even frailer than the last, and Shafer recognized the voice to be that of an elderly woman: frail, scratchy.

He fought past the pain in his knee, blinking water from his eyes, and stood again. Meanwhile, an announcement blared over the boat's speakers: "Ladies and gentlemen, boarding will be closed until the storm blows through. If you are onboard the ship, please return to your cabin. Thank you."

"Hang on," Shafer yelled, but water rushed into his mouth and he fell into a sputtering, coughing fit. Spewing it out, he shook his head and continued climbing.

As he finally stumbled to the top of the stairs, the intercom came back on. "Ladies and gentlemen, if you need any assistance, our staff will be coming around. Look for them in the hallways. Because of the severity of the boat's pitching, no more passengers will be allowed to board or exit the *Delta Voyager*."

"Yeah, I got it," Shafer muttered as he looked around the top deck. "Hey, is that a basketball court?" It was, and it was just as water-soaked as everything else. The court was surrounded by a chain-link cage, which he ran to and grabbed a hold of while the boat was briefly level.

"Hello?" He called out. "Ma'am?"

A weak response came: "Please… help me."

With his hair matted to his face and beads of water streaming down his cheeks, Shafer peered through the onslaught of rain, desperately searching for the woman behind the voice.

When he saw her, his heart nearly skipped a beat.

Shafer was right about a couple of things: the woman was old, with curly white hair that was soaking wet. She was also desperate, looking frantic and terrified.

What he hadn't expected, however, was that the woman was also in a wheelchair.

And she was holding on for dear life.

As he moved closer to assess the situation, walking his hands down the chain-link fence, Shafer began to take in the rain-assaulted scene. The woman was under an awning and she was clutching onto a rail as the boat rocked back and forth. A book was tucked into her lap.

"I… I was up here reading while Hughey went down to the cabin to take a nap," she said through choppy breaths. "I fell asleep, and when I woke up…"

"Don't worry," Shafer tried to console her as he clutched onto the cage. "Just hang on. I'm going to come get you. It's gonna be okay."

As he spoke, the ship rocked harder than ever and Shafer's feet nearly slid out from under him. The book in the woman's lap fell to the deck, only to be swept up in a current of water and washed to the railing of the ship, then flipped off the deck with a violent splash. It plummeted out of sight, diving to the dark, choppy waters below.

"I can't hold on for much longer," she pleaded. "I'm slipping…"

"On my way," Shafer said, shuffling his way along the cage. Once the ship leveled out again, he made a dash to the far side of the cage, only an arm's length away from the woman. Before he made it to her, though, another pitch of the deck sent him sliding into the fence.

"Young man!" A shout came from behind him. "Stay there. I'll save you."

Shafer turned back towards the steps to see a Latino man fighting to keep his balance as he climbed them. He wore a crewmember uniform and was trying to also wear a brave face, but unsuccessfully.

"I don't need saving," Shafer shot back. "It's not *me* that I'm worried about! Somebody should have come to check the top deck…"

"That's why I'm here," the deckhand shouted back over the storm. "I'll grab a… a… life preserver!"

Shafer rolled his eyes as the boat leveled out. "Or, how about we actually stop this woman here from falling and needing one?"

As the speakers chimed on once again, repeating the request for passengers to stay in their rooms, a fourth voice hollered out, "Shafer?"

Shafer recognized this voice immediately. "Stuart, over here!" He called back just as the ship rocked back in the other direction. Again he lost his footing, slipping and clutching onto the cage. If it wasn't for the chain-link, he would have been heading straight into the deck's railing.

The woman, however, was not as fortunate. Unlike Shafer, she hadn't managed to keep her grip, and with a terrified scream, her hands peeled off the handrail. As she flailed desperately, her wheelchair began to skid toward the railing.

"Help!" she shouted. "Help!"

"Dammit," Shafer muttered as he quickly looked around. He needed a rope. He needed something to reach her, to keep her from going over. But he had nothing. Nothing at all, which only left him with one option.

With a shaky sigh, Shafer let go of the fence. At once, he began to slide down the deck, pursuing the woman. Vaguely, he registered Mr. Brimley shouting his name, but he wasn't focused on that. All he could think about was the burbling surface of the ocean ten stories below him.

The deckhand, frozen in disbelief, yelled, "Young man!"

As the woman continued to scream, Shafer bent his knees and widened his stance. With a low center of gravity, he felt like he was surfing, just without the board... or any pretense of control.

The one thing he did have, however, was speed. In an instant, he was right behind the woman, who reached out to him with a pleading look in her eyes.

"Hold on," he said again, bracing for impact with the rail.

With that, two things happened so close together he wasn't sure which came first. For one, the ship began to level out, giving Mr. Brimley and the deckhand an opportunity to charge forward. Meanwhile, both Shafer and the woman struck the railing. Just before their collision, he'd managed to grab onto one side of her wheelchair, pulling against it just enough to keep her from tumbling out or flipping over the rails.

That effort, however, had left Shafer unprepared to absorb the contact. He slammed into the rail with enough momentum that he lost his balance, and despite his best efforts to lean back towards the ship, he flipped over the railing with a shout.

As soon as his feet left the deck, time slowed. Rain pelted down on him as he blindly flailed his arms, trying to grab onto something. Below him, the ocean swelled and reached up to grab him, slapping the sides of the ship with murky waves.

The water was ready to absorb him, to suck him in and never let him go.

But Shafer wasn't ready for that. Just as he crested and began to plummet toward the ocean below, he somehow managed to grab onto the railing with his right hand. As he brought up his other hand for support, his body slammed into the side of the ship, knocking all the air from his lungs. Gasping, he held on for dear life as the sway of the ship and intensity of the rain did everything possible to pry him loose.

His grip was giving way. One by one, his fingers were slipping off the rail.

The woman reached out for him, but there was nothing she could do.

Fortunately, help came from another place.

"Shafer!" Mr. Brimley yelled, reaching around the railing and grabbing Shafer by his wrists. "I've got you, Shafer."

Still dangling above the water, Shafer let out a big sigh of relief. "Good timing." He cut his eyes to the lady in the wheelchair. "She needs help…"

"I've got her," said the deckhand, grabbing onto the wheelchair while the deck was level. "Ma'am, I'm going to get you to the elevator."

As the ocean continued to violently churn beneath

DELTA ADRIFT

Shafer, Mr. Brimley asked, "Can you climb up?"

With a nod and grunt of effort, Shafer kicked a leg up, wrapping it around the railing. From there, he pulled the rest of his weight up and over the railing, which he and Mr. Brimley both held onto as the ship rocked back in the other direction.

Once he was safe , Shafer panted, "That was a close one." Squinting through the storm at Mr. Brimley, he added, "You saved me. How did you know..?"

"I saw you take off out of the bathroom so I figured something must be wrong."

"Are May and Heather in the room?"

"Yeah, I told them we'd be there shortly. May was worried about you, though—she's convinced you're always putting yourself in harm's way."

Shafer didn't respond. Deep down, he knew she was right. Just now, once again he'd risked his life.

Questions swirled through his head like the water at his feet: *Why was he like this? Was there something wrong with him? Did he enjoy the rush of adventure so much that he sought it out, or was it all just coincidence?*

And, perhaps the biggest question of all: *What if he hadn't done it?*

Another boom of thunder clapped in the sky and lightning briefly illuminated the dark clouds outside, pulling Shafer from his deep thoughts. The boat leveled out again, and together he and Mr. Brimley hurried under the awning, toward the elevator.

Once they'd made it inside, Shafer shook his head, looking down at his soaked clothes and ruined shoes as his heart still raced in his chest. "Hey, Stuart?"

"Yes?"

"Do you think May would believe me if I told her I just wanted to take a selfie on the basketball court?"

Mr. Brimley smiled and shook his head. "No way."

"Yeah, figured..." He let out a sigh. "She's not gonna be happy."

"It's a tradeoff," Mr. Brimley said as he put a hand on Shafer's shoulder.

"What do you mean?"

The ship rocked once again. "If you care about somebody, you want them safe, but you also have to respect their decisions as well. Do you think Mary Jane *wanted* Peter Parker to go on all his dangerous missions?"

With water running down into his eyes, Shafer shook his head. "No. Of course not. She just knew that's how it works."

"Then May will learn to do the same thing," Mr. Brimley replied. "That's what comes with dating a superhero, and Shafer, let me tell you, I'm convinced you're just that."

ELEVEN: OPEN-AIR

"Wait, he said *what* about Spider-Man?" May's voice was equal parts irritated and confused.

"I mean, basically what I just said, but it made more sense when your dad said it." Shafer turned to look at May, who sat beside him on his bed, but there was an icy distance between them. "You need to work with me here. I'm pretty sure your parents went to the late-night ice sculpting just so we could have a little time to talk... so talk to me."

She sighed. "For one, no. My dad's a big nerd and totally would want to go see ice get sculpted anyway. And two, why would I talk to you if I don't know how long I'm going to be able to?"

"May..."

"Shafer, think about it." She refused to look his way. "I've never liked a boy like I like you. And I know we haven't known each other for very long, but like you said yesterday, we just kinda clicked."

"Wait." Shafer looked at the TV, which was playing silently across the room. "I know you're mad at me, so why did that sound like a string of compliments?"

May huffed out an irritated sigh. "For someone so clever, you're also so stupid. If I cared about you—like *really* cared about you—why might I have a problem with you constantly seeking out near-death experiences?"

"I get it. You want me to be safe. You don't want anything to happen to me." He looked at her again, debating if he should reach out and put an arm around her. He wanted to hold her, but also knew she could strike at any moment like a venomous snake.

"If you get it, then *stop doing it*," she pleaded. Her voice quivered for a moment, but then she coughed and fought back tears. "I understand what happened during our trip. The kidnapping. The robots. The bomb. All of that. That doesn't bug me. Not like this, at least."

"Why not? That doesn't make—"

"Because you didn't *seek* it out," she cut in. "Stuff happened to you, but it was all so coincidental, and it's honestly just a miracle you survived."

Shafer knew he probably should tread lightly, but he couldn't help himself. He asked, "So what you're saying is fighting an army of robots is okay, but I should have declined your dad's offer to drive his new car-- which I didn't even know was malfunctioning, by the way--, and I should have completely ignored a desperate lady who was pleading for help?"

May didn't respond, only stared at the muted television.

"May, I didn't *look* for any of it. What happened earlier only happened to me because I was the only person in earshot, and not because I was out searching for things to do, but because *I went to the bathroom.*"

Suddenly, a single tear dropped from the corner of May's eye, rolling down her cheek and to her chin. She sniffled and wiped it away.

"May..." Shafer pleaded. "Listen to me. I'm not *trying* to do anything to upset you. I'm not *trying* to risk my life, or—"

"Shafer, I'm sorry," she said. This time her voice was weak.

"You're... sorry?"

She was crying now. Full-out crying. Big tears. "I'm sorry. You're right."

"I'm... wait, what?"

More tears came, which she wiped away. "You're right, Shafer. You are, and I'm just being selfish. I know that you're not trying to go seek out the spotlight. I know you're not trying to save little ol' ladies because you like being a hero and because you want to waste four straight hours filling out accident reports."

"That was *super* annoying," Shafer tossed in.

"Yeah," she nodded, still crying. "I get that, and I don't know what I'm even mad at you for, honestly, but more than anything I'm just scared. I'm scared something will happen. I'm scared that someday you *won't* pull off the next heroic adventure. I'm scared of losing you, Shafer, because I care. I care so damn much about you, and I don't know what I'd do if I didn't have you."

"May, you're funny and beautiful. You're smart and sweet. You could find *anybody.*"

"I know that was supposed to be a compliment, but it's not helping," she said with a laugh through her tears. "I don't want anybody, I want *you*."

"So what do you want me to do?" He looked at her again, and this time she finally looked back.

They held gazes for a moment, neither speaking.

Then, after the moment of silence, she said, "Just be Shafer McCartney. I like you because of you, so don't try to be a hero. Don't try to be… I don't know, the *Golden Ocelot*."

He smirked.

"But also don't change," May continued. "That's not what I'm asking for. I like you because of how you are." She looked down for just a moment, wiping away another tear but offering a soft smile. "Just never forget that you have other people that care about you, too. Next time you're doing one of your stupid stunts, remember how many people will miss you if something goes wrong."

"May…" He held her gaze. "If you think that, even for a second, you're not always in the back of my mind, then you're wrong. When I was holding onto that railing, it's like you were there with me. And maybe it's selfish of me, but I don't want anything to happen to me because I haven't finished writing my story with you."

Arching an eyebrow, she asked, "Wait… what about the railing?"

Suddenly remembering he'd left that particular detail out during his retelling of the adventure, he backtracked. "Um, nothing. Just know that you're always going to be with me in my head."

Fortunately, that answer seemed good enough for May. She said, "If you can promise me that, then save all

the old ladies you want."
"You got a deal."

*****

Shafer rubbed his eyes and looked at the clock beside his bed. It was two in the morning. Everything was quiet. Everything was still despite vivid dreams of being pitched around.

He got up, walked to the bathroom, and got a drink. Then, laying back down in his bed, he attempted to fall back asleep. He tried to turn off his brain, but as he lay there, staring up at his ceiling, sleep refused to come.

The longer he laid in bed, the more awake he felt. He ended up playing a game on his phone for a few minutes, hoping to lull himself back to sleep. It didn't work. So, deciding sleep wasn't coming anytime soon, Shafer slipped into his sneakers, ran a comb through his hair, and wandered out of his room.

As soon as he was outside, he realized he'd forgotten his hat, but in the middle of the night, surely he would be okay without it.

He thought about texting May. If she was awake, she'd want to join, but he guessed she was asleep. They'd bade each other good night a couple of hours ago, and she needed the rest. She'd had a stressful day, after all, worrying about him as he nearly died. That's how she'd put it, right?

As he passed the door of the Brimley's room, he stopped for just a moment. It was completely silent inside. *Everything* was silent, save the occasional groan of the ship.

"It's a huge boat," he whispered to himself as he started down the hall once again. "Surely there's *something* for me to do."

The dive-in theater had stopped playing a bit ago. The midnight snacks had probably passed too, but he wasn't hungry.

A thought popped into his head: The hot tubs! They were open twenty-four-seven, right? Sure, he didn't have a swimsuit, but he could just go check and see if he could get in one. Relaxing in a hot tub, staring up at the stars, and cruising through the middle of the Atlantic? Not a bad way to spend an hour.

More than anything, there would be peace and quiet.

He slipped into the serenity spa, which had signs posted stating no minors were allowed, but he didn't think his under-agedness would be a problem at 2 in the morning. It should be empty, just him, the water, and the sky full of bright stars.

Or, at least he thought.

As he approached the hot tub, he saw two heads poking out of the water. Two females. Two *younger* females. Two younger females who were very *attractive* females, at that.

Instantly, Shafer began to second-guess this idea. What would May think if she saw him here? Sure, his intentions were innocent, but she wouldn't have any way of knowing that. Nobody would.

Playing it safe, he decided it would be best to turn around and go back. There were other hot tubs and there were other things to do, for sure. He could lay on the lido deck in a pool chair and look up at the stars. He'd never noticed them as bright as they were out here.

But as Shafer turned around to slip away, the chit-chat of the two girls in the pool turned into a direct question. "No way. You're... are you Shafer McCartney?"

It was a half-statement, half question, and it came from the girl on the right. He turned back to the hot tub, instantly regretting not wearing his hat.

"Um, hey there."

"No freaking way," the other girl whispered to the first. "I didn't believe you."

"I told you! I def told you."

Shafer was caught in the cross-fire. He was half-tempted to leave while the girls went back and forth, but then the taller girl climbed out of the tub. She was slim with blonde hair that hit the middle of her shoulder blades.

"It is like... *crazy* to meet you," she said, trying to adjust her hair. "I'm Ashley."

Her friend, not to be outdone, followed her closely. She was even prettier than Ashley, with olive skin and dark eyes. She wasn't tall and had an eloquent hourglass figure. "I'm Breanna."

"Yeah, hey," Shafer offered weakly. "I was just making a quick round, and..."

They closed in fast. Ashley said, "I'm nineteen, and I go to FSU. We both do. I'm an art history major."

"And *I'm* a chemical engineer," Breanna said like she was trying to win an important job.

"Um... cool," Shafer looked back and forth between the two of them. "I'm in high school. And yeah, that's about it. I'm here with my girlfriend."

"Oh, that's cool." Ashley pressed. "May, right?"

"Yeah," he nodded, trying not to seem uncomfortable. "I was about to go see her."

Ashley sounded a bit skeptical. "Where *is* your girlfriend?

"In her room."

"You guys have different rooms?"

"Yeah, her parents booked me an extra one. They're great. Got me my own suite."

"A *suite?* No way. Can we like… go see your room?" Ashley pushed. "Can we Shafer? Please?"

He shook his head. "Not a good idea, I'm sorry. I just was going to come here and…" he trailed off, desperately searching for a good excuse, and then he blurted out the first thing that came out of his mouth: "I was going to go visit with the captain." He regretted saying it immediately.

"You know the *captain?*" Breanna sounded impressed. "You're *so* famous, Shafer."

"I'll be a has-been before you know it," he said while forcing a smile. "It was nice talking to you."

"Can we have your number?" Ashley asked.

"Uh… I don't give my number to strangers, I'm sorry."

"That's cool," Breanna said, a little more sympathetic. "But hey, can I get a picture with you first?"

"Yeah, me too!" Ashley chirped.

Shafer began to feel guilty. He wasn't used to telling people no, and he'd already turned them down with his phone number. How could he say no to something as simple as one picture?

…But how could he say yes?

He'd promised May that he was done—no more fan

pictures for the cruise. And what if he took this one? What if she found out? A picture in the middle of the night with two bikini-clad college girls. That was a picture that would tell a story on its own.

As politely as he could, Shafer raised both hands in front of him and said, "Listen, nothing against you guys at all—you're great, I'm sure—but I promised myself and I promised May that I'm done taking pictures with 'fans' or whatever, at least for the rest of the cruise. I'm trying to be normal and have a normal vacation. You get that, right?"

Breanna nodded.

Ashley looked surprised she'd been turned down, and Shafer didn't know what else to say, but Breanna saved the day. "That's cool. We get it. And hey, if you were coming to meet with the captain, Shafer, there he goes now."

Shafer spun around to see a man in all white slipping through the door that led to the elevator. The timing couldn't have been better. "Oh, uh... yeah! Thanks. I nearly missed him. I'll see you around for sure."

With that, he was gone, leaving the two girls on the serenity deck and following behind the captain.

"That was lucky," he mumbled to himself. *Who would have thought that his half-baked excuse would have actually worked so well?*

He hurried to the door, making a point to look like he was actually following the captain, but his new plan was to head back to his room as soon as he was out of the girls' sight. He'd get in his bed and lay there until he fell asleep. Late-night excursions weren't such a great idea, after all.

Maybe his fame would be tougher to escape than he'd ever expected.

Relief swept over him as he made his way inside the hall and out of the ocean air.

But as the door silently slid shut behind him, he had a strange feeling.

Something was wrong.

With one look at the captain, Shafer knew his plan might not work out the way he'd hoped. He could tell he might be in for more than he ever expected.

TWELVE:
BEHIND THE VEIL

Shafer had developed a sixth sense.

He wasn't sure where it came from. Or *when* he'd gotten it, for that matter. He wasn't sure if he wanted it. But he knew he had it, and he knew that, whether he liked it or not, he was stuck with it.

It was the ability to tell when something was off. To look at a person and, judging by his or her demeanor, know something was not right. Perhaps it had come from too much exposure to deception and corruption.

Too much practice.

But for whatever reason, Shafer knew immediately that the captain of the ship was up to something. The first tell was his gait. He moved like he was trying to be stealthy and discreet.

"Probably shouldn't be wearing all white," Shafer mused under his breath as he watched the captain creep down the hall, quickly looking back and forth between the doors on each side of the hall.

After watching for just a bit longer, Shafer determined something else: This man wasn't Captain Graf. He was much larger, more muscular. This was the captain-in-training, or whatever he was called.

Captain Szalay.

Szalay slinked forward. He wore a backpack over one shoulder, and it rocked back and forth with his movements. He reached the end of the hall and darted to his left, out of sight.

Shafer stood in the door, watching as Szalay disappeared and debating what he should do.

It's probably fine, he told himself. *Surely he's just going back to his room. He's probably going to change, go to bed, and leave the ship on auto-pilot or something.*

Even as he thought the words, he knew they were false. Try as he might, he couldn't convince himself that everything was okay, or that there *was* a perfectly good reason for Szalay to be sneaking around the upper decks in the middle of the night. From the way he was walking to the way he looked nervous, none of it made sense.

Shafer should've been in bed. His room was just down the hall, and he could still turn a blind eye and call it a night. Surely everything would be fine in the morning.

But he didn't have it in him. He wasn't wired that way. Try as he might, he couldn't unsee what he'd just witnessed, and his body was walking forward before his brain could ever override the action.

"C'mon, Shafer," he scolded himself. "What are you doing? Just go back to your room. Go to bed."

His words did no good. When he reached the first

bend of the hall, he peeked around the corner in the direction that Szalay had disappeared.

Sure enough, Szalay was still there, acting even more suspicious than before. He was standing beside a door and fiddling with keys. He looked further down the hallway, checking to see if the coast was clear, and then he looked the other way.

Quickly, Shafer ducked out of sight. *Had he been seen?* His heart raced as he listened intently. There were several moments of silence, then a very faint sound of keys rattling.

Shafer exhaled, thankful.

A few seconds later, hinges squeaked. At the sound, Shafer peered around his cover and watched Szalay slip through the door, closing it behind him.

Except, it didn't close. Not quite.

Szalay had left it cracked.

As Shafer peered at the two inches of darkness between the door and the frame, he told himself to let it go, that closure to the mystery wasn't worth sneaking around.

But he also knew he couldn't help himself. If Szalay hadn't bothered to close it behind him, Shafer *had* to check it out.

May was right. Maybe something *was* wrong with him, after all. Maybe, despite everything he'd said to her—everything he'd been saying to himself, at that—he *did* like the thrill of adventure. Maybe he couldn't help but seek it out. It was built into him, coded into his DNA. He couldn't leave any stone unturned, compelled by curiosity, stupidity, or something in between.

Once again, Shafer willed himself to stop, but his body didn't listen. He ventured forward, and now he was the one looking anxiously over both shoulders, making sure he was all alone.

He wasn't.

A door creaked open in front of him, and Shafer froze in his tracks. A heavyset man with a bald head and thick mustache lumbered into the hallway. He was wearing an enormous blue robe, looking only half-awake.

When he spotted Shafer, he asked, "Hey buddy. D'ya know if the late-night snacks are still open?"

"I don't," Shafer whispered back. "Sorry."

The man nodded but looked like he was still processing the words. Foggy-eyed, he strolled past Shafer, disappearing down the hall.

Shafer stood there for a moment, letting his heart rate calm from the surprise. He pretended to look at the ship's map that hung on the wall.

Then, once the man was out of sight, he reverted back to sleuth-mode. He crept to the cracked door, noticing a sign on it: *Staff Only*. Peering through the crack, Shafer tried to spot Szalay through the darkness, but the captain was nowhere to be seen. Just a dimly lit room, a lot bigger than he expected.

"Where did he go?" Shafer muttered. He looked back at the sign hanging on the door one last time. If he snuck behind doors that were closed to passengers, he was crossing the point of no return.

One last time, Shafer questioned what he was doing, if he should let it go. His room, by now, was only a few doors away. It wouldn't take any effort to get back in his bed. To close his eyes and try to forget any of this happened.

But that would never work. Not for him. "Sorry,

May," he muttered, then, overpowered by his curiosity, he cracked open the door and snuck inside, taking a few steps into the room and following the light.

The room was nothing at all what he expected.

For one thing, it was not as much a room as it was another hallway, just as long as the one he'd come from, but significantly skinnier. It was darker too, lit only with bare lightbulbs hanging from the ceiling at distant but consistent intervals. Pipes, ducts, and wires ran from ceiling to floor.

This must be the plumbing and electric, Shafer thought as he took everything in. He'd flushed the over-powered toilet several times but never once considered where it went while they were on the ship.

As he peered down the shadowy hall, from the cement floor to the pipes and ducts winding around the ceiling and walls, the luxury of the cruise ship was a distant memory. No longer was he in a swanky hallway—this felt more like a cave.

And down the hall, Shafer could make out Szaley's hulking figure, the backpack still hanging from one shoulder. He stepped over a duct, moving with purpose. Then, after a pause, Szalay took a phone from the pocket of his white captain's pants, stopping only long enough to punch a few buttons and hold it to his ear.

There's no chance he gets any signal down here, Shafer thought. *In the middle of the ocean and in a sketchy hallway—what's he thinking?*

"Hello?" Szalay greeted only a few seconds later.

I stand corrected, Shafer told himself.

The captain said a few more words, but this time he was whispering. Shafer was out of earshot, especially given the occasional groan of the pipes as the ship gently pitched. If he wanted to find out what was going on, he had to get closer.

Hunkering down, he snuck forward, making sure to step on his heels then roll his feet to reduce the noise he made on the cold cement. Perhaps even more importantly, he had to know exactly where his body was, too. Kicking a pipe or bumping into a shadowy air duct would instantly give him away.

Szalay stopped walking again, looking at a sign on his right while continuing his phone call. This gave Shafer the opportunity he needed, and he slipped behind a cluster of pipes, just out of Szalay's sight.

Szalay was still whispering, but his words carried through the chamber. "Just a status report." A pause. "No, nothing's wrong. Everything's going well. It's about to be done."

What is he talking about? From the shadows, Shafer squinted at Szalay, trying to take in every little detail of the scene. The first thing he noticed was the phone. It wasn't a smartphone, but something thicker. Bulkier. Something that looked less advanced.

The backpack was the next thing that caught Shafer's eye, but not because of its simple green-and-black design. Instead, something *else* drew his interest. The bag had a bulge at the very bottom, and the way it swung as Szalay suggested that whatever was inside had quite a bit of weight to it.

Shafer was even more confused now, and the phone conversation didn't help. "I've got to admit, this is an impressive device," Szalay said. "I had my doubts about this."

A momentary pause came, then a very faint response came from the other end of the conversation.

"No, I'm at the room now. Your blueprints were spot on." Another pause. "Yes, Klaw."

Klaw? What kind of name was that? Shafer didn't have much time to ponder, as Szalay's next response added even more confusion.

"Yes, the boy is fine. He's in a separate room. Different ducts. It made all of this very easy."

At this, there was a click of recognition in Shafer's brain. He still had no idea what was going on, but something about Szalay's words sounded too familiar: if they were talking about a boy in a separate room on this deck of the ship, he had a good guess what "boy" they had meant.

They were talking about *him*.

But why? What did Szalay want with Shafer? He was on a cruise! He'd left the stealth and danger behind on the mainland, or at least he'd thought.

Szalay only provided more confusion as he wrapped up the call. "I'll call you after it's finished," he said, then hung up the phone and took off the backpack. Very carefully, he set it down on the cement floor directly under a bare lightbulb, then unzipped it.

The ship swayed again, making all the pipes groan at once. Spooked, Szalay glanced down both sides of the hall, forcing Shafer to press himself against the wall.

After a few seconds, Szalay resumed his work and Shafer resumed watching him.

In Shafer's head, there was a "big reveal" coming for whatever was in the backpack, but the anticipation far outweighed the reality. The object Szalay extracted from the bag was a small, rectangular device that Shafer did not recognize in the slightest.

Szalay turned to the wall behind him, the device in hand, and examined a sign hanging below the ducts. It was small, only containing two characters: *9-B.*

Shafer recognized the characters immediately. Suite 9-B was the room May and her parents were staying in. Shafer was right beside them, in 9-A.

Szalay, looking confident that he was in the right place, set the metal device down and dug a screwdriver from his bag. He followed a duct just a few feet to the right, reaching a flat metal panel, which he purposefully began to unscrew. After a bit of work, he removed it altogether and carefully placed it flat on the floor.

Very few times in his life had Shafer been more confused than now. Along with the confusion came questions about how Shafer should handle the situation: should he give away his hiding spot and confront Szalay, or should he watch and see where this goes?

For the time being, Shafer elected to stay tucked away in the shadows. *If* foul play was going on, he didn't want to show his hand too early.

Szalay picked up the metal device, carefully examined it, then he pushed a button on the side of it.

Shafer tensed.

Szalay tensed, too.

The device responded to the touch by issuing a very low hum and then emitting something into the air. Was it a vaper? A smoke? A fog? Something in between. The mist was barely visible in the air, but Shafer could just make it out as he strained his eyes in the dimly lit chamber.

DELTA ADRIFT

As soon as the machine began to smoke, Szalay carefully slid it through the opening he'd created in the duct, setting it down as quietly as possible.

That's when Shafer noticed something that *really* made him nervous.

It was Szalay's face. His jaw was tight, his nostrils were flared, his lips were pursed, and his neck was rigid—he was holding his breath.

And if Szalay was holding his breath as he handled this device—a device he'd just placed in the vents—it was because he didn't want to breathe in the mist. In some way or another, it must be dangerous. Toxic. Poisonous.

And then, as Szalay picked up the metal panel from the cement floor and prepared to seal the duct, his intentions became resoundingly clear: for some reason, he was trying to flood the Brimley's suite with this dangerous toxin.

Shafer couldn't let that happen.

Cat-like, he crept out of the shadows and positioned himself right behind Szalay, who was carefully lining up the panel and preparing to seal the duct back as he'd found it.

He never finished.

Instead, Shafer's fist slammed into the side of the man's head.

Szalay, taken by complete surprise, didn't have time to brace for the impact. His neck jolted violently to the side. He stumbled, tripping over a pipe, and collapsed to the floor. The metal panel fell as well, clattering to the cement and sending an echo through the chamber.

His hand throbbing, Shafer unfurled his fist and shook out the pain as his eyes fell on the motionless body sprawled on the cement floor. Then, once the feeling returned to his hand, he quickly bent down and peered into the duct while holding his breath.

The misting device was sitting freely on the cold metal, so Shafer quickly snatched it. It was heavier than he expected, and all the smoke was coming from one end, so he pointed that end away as he turned it around in his hand.

Where's the off switch? He thought as he looked over the fancy dials and meters.

Not seeing one, he decided on a different approach. With both hands, he hoisted it overhead and then slammed it down into the concrete. There was a triumphant crack as the device broke into several pieces. The humming stopped immediately, as did the mist. A pool of cloudy liquid ran from underneath the busted device

Shafer looked down at what he'd done, taking in his work. "Who needs an off switch?"

As an answer, huge hands suddenly wrapped around him and shoved him into the concrete wall.

Caught off guard, Shafer barely managed to lift an arm in time to protect his face, but he caught his forearm on the edge of a duct, shooting a razor of pain down his body. He spun from the wall, only to see a dazed-but-angry Szalay standing in the middle of the chamber.

"How the hell did you get down here?" The words were a growl.

"I'll tell you if you tell me why you're trying to gas the Brimley's," Shafer countered.

"That's none of your business."

"Then you're getting nothing from me."

Szalay looked even more enraged as he glared down

at the broken device on the cement floor. "How dare you!"

Shafer didn't manage a response before Szalay dove forward, grabbing him by the shoulders and shoving him back into the wall. Then, through gritted teeth, he muttered, "This isn't a very fair fight. You're huge."

It was true. Szalay was at least a head taller and easily outweighed Shafer by sixty or seventy pounds. The large man's muscles rippled under his white uniform.

"You should have considered that before you punched me," Szalay growled.

"Yeah, at this point, I'd agree with that," Shafer wheezed as he was pressed even harder into the wall.

Instead of carrying on the conversation any longer, Shafer drew up one leg and lashed out with a kick, striking Szalay square in the chest. Szalay stumbled backward, but not before grabbing onto Shafer's foot and pulling him down, too.

Shafer landed on top of the large man, but it took no time at all for Szaley to roll and pin Shafer, drawing back a fist and throwing a hard punch at the boy's face.

Shafer jerked his head out of the way, narrowly dodging the blow, and Szalay struck the floor. He bellowed in pain, and then, spotting something beside him, he reached out with one hand while keeping Shafer pinned down with the other.

When Shafer identified what Szaley had grabbed, his heart nearly stopped. It was the screwdriver, which glinted in the faint light of the bare bulb overhead. Szalay's beefy hand wrapped around the handle and the shank was pointed straight down at Shafer's neck. It began to lower.

Shafer grabbed onto the man's arm and tried with every ounce of strength to fight back, but it was no use. Closer and closer it came to Shafer's throat. This was it. This was the end. But then, Szalay stopped. He looked to the screwdriver, then to Shafer, and then lowered it.

With a huff, he said, "Let the record show that I would have killed you here and now, Shafer McCartney, but I've been told by the boss that I can't."

Out of everything going on in his head, Shafer managed to say, "That's... nice?"

"I suppose." Szalay laughed again. "But don't get cocky. He said I couldn't kill you, but he didn't say I can't do *this*..." As the words left his mouth, Szalay clamped his huge hand around Shafer's neck.

Suddenly, all airflow was lost. An all-too-familiar feeling was back: Shafer was suffocating, and there was no air to be found.

He jerked. He kicked. He did everything in his power to shake Szalay off of him, but there was no use. Szalay was too big. Too strong.

Shafer's vision flickered as his body cried out for air. He pleaded, incoherent words babbling from his mouth, but relief never came.

Air never came.

Shafer's vision left him first, and his consciousness followed quickly behind.

THIRTEEN:
THE SAND NECKTIE

Shafer's skull weighed a thousand pounds. His head sagged forward and his eyes refused to open.

The first thing he noticed was the smell. Salty. Tropical. Oceanic.

He could feel something around him, too. It was relaxing. Peaceful. Gentle pressure surrounding him and supporting him, kind of like a sleeping bag. Except he wasn't lying down. He was upright.

The world around him was alive with sounds. First, he made out the splash of waves rolling. The crash of the waves and froth of the ocean sounded close. *Very* close. There were birds, too. Gulls, from the sound of it.

He forced his eyes open.

Sand. Lots of sand. And it was right in front of his face, only inches from his nose.

"What the hell?" He leaned his head back, squinting in the early morning light as he waited for his eyes to adjust. They didn't. Groaning, he shut them again.

After a moment, he opened his eyes once more, and this time he saw the ocean. It stretched out as far as he could see, waves rolling to the horizon. As they churned and chopped, every single wave caught a sliver of the morning sun and the orange and pink sky.

"Where am I?" His words barely left his mouth. "How did I get here?"

Something else caught Shafer's eye. A boat. It was in the distance, sailing across the sunny horizon. He blinked a couple of times and focused on it. It was huge. More than a boat. It was a ship—a cruise ship.

At that point, puzzlement turned into discovery: it wasn't just any cruise ship—it was the *Delta Voyager*, he was sure of it. But if the ship was out there, where was he? How had he gotten here?

All at once, the memories rushed back: what he'd seen. What he'd done. Szalay's strong hands gripping around his throat.

Suddenly, all the grogginess fled, and, fully coherent, he realized that he was in trouble. *Big* trouble.

The sensation that he'd first taken as a warm embrace now gave him a different feeling: restriction. He'd been mistaken. He wasn't being held and supported. No. He was trapped and couldn't move.

His eyes watered as they adjusted to the light, but he forced them to stay open nonetheless, taking in his surroundings. He looked down at the sand once again, and this time he pieced everything together.

Shafer was buried. He'd been buried alive.

DELTA ADRIFT

The sand was up to his neck, scraping against the bottom of his chin. Under the surface, his palms were held together with even tighter pressure wrapped around his wrist. They had been bound together, he was sure of it.

He couldn't move. Even worse, he could barely breathe as sand pressed into his diaphragm and the ocean waves lapped up to the beach, spraying mist in his face.

He tried to shake loose, jerking his body back and forth. The sand didn't budge. It was damp and packed in tightly enough that it might as well have been cement.

With his heart racing, Shafer forced himself to take a deep breath, or at least as deep as he could before the sand restricted his chest. *Think, Shafer, think.* He looked around the beach.

To his right was a pile of sand, freshly upturned. There were shoeprints, too, pressed into the damp sand all around him. Somebody had put in a lot of effort just to bury him.

One more thing caught his eye, halfway up the beach and nearly hidden behind the pile of sand: a boat. A motorboat. It was small, wooden, and tied down to a short post, rising and falling in the waves. *Is this boat how he'd gotten here? How did he get off the ship?*

"Ah, you're up." The voice came from behind him. It was a strange mix of chipper and smug. It was Szalay.

"Yeah. I'm really *digging* this view," Shafer shot back.

The footsteps approached, softly crunching through the sand.

Trying to get a response, Shafer added, "Nothing like waking up to a beautiful view of the ocean."

"I kinda like you, kid. You're ballsy." The voice was

even closer now, and after a few seconds, Szalay came into view. He looked much different now, though. No longer was he wearing a captain's uniform, but instead looked dressed for combat, including dark boots and a black bulletproof vest over a white tank top.

Szalay was carrying something, too—a lawn chair. It was old and weathered, but it held the large man's weight when he unfolded it and staked it into the sand in front of Shafer. The big man had a black eye, so swollen that it was almost shut.

Shafer said, "Wow, you look like hell."

"Coming from the boy who's stuck neck-deep in sand."

"Good one." Shafer tried to writhe around, but once again to no avail. "Listen, Szalay, I'm one of those people that likes talking with my hands, and that's kinda hard to do given my current predicament, so if you want to have a good conversation, you should get me outta here."

Szalay laughed. "Don't get ahead of yourself. I'm not here to make friends. I just want to chat for a minute before I go to town. I've got to send out a message."

"Town? Message?" Shafer had a thousand questions. "What do you mean? What town? Where are we?"

"Doesn't matter," Szalay dismissed all the questions at once. He leaned back in the chair, reaching over an armrest and tracing his fingers through the sand.

"You gotta tell me! That's how the villain's great reveal works. At least play along..."

Szalay sighed, annoyed. "Fine. We are on a small island where we docked last night for an hour to pick up a few medical supplies."

"I didn't know the ship was stopping."

DELTA ADRIFT

"None of the passengers did. Most of them will never realize we did. They'll wake up to more open water."

The morning sun was right behind Szalay's head, so Shafer averted his eyes out to the *Delta Voyager*, which was growing further away with every passing second. He began to fire away more questions. "Why are you here? Who are you? Why are you doing this to me?"

Szalay held up a hand. "Shafer, relax. One at a time, please."

"Tell me who you are, Szalay. I'm guessing you're no captain-in-training."

He shook his head. "You're correct, Shafer. And my name isn't Szalay—it's Ash."

"What were you doing on the ship, *Ash?*"

Ash glanced over his shoulder, out to the *Delta Voyager*. "A job."

"What kind of... wait." Shafer realized the answer before he ever said it. "You're a... hitman?"

"A contract killer, yeah," Ash confirmed, sharing the info just as casually as if he were a teacher or an engineer.

"Sorry, I didn't realize there was a politically correct version. Hope I didn't upset you."

Ash huff-laughed. "And I'm actually doing a job for another person in the same line of work, who is doing the job for somebody else."

"Wow, cool." Shafer tried to move his arms again, but they refused to budge. "You're a hitman... working for a lazy hitman."

"Not a lazy one," Ash shook his head. "A *legendary* one. The best to do it. We're talking about the Michael Jordan of contract killers."

"You mean the LeBron?"

Ash rolled his eyes. "I'm talking about a man who never fails on a hit. He always delivers. A perfect track record."

"Then why are you here?"

"Because of you, Shafer."

"Huh?"

Ash chuckled. "Klaw had to bring me in on the job because, quite frankly, he failed."

Klaw. The name struck a note in Shafer's mind. He remembered it from Ash's phone conversation. "What? How did it fail?"

Ash corrected himself. "His *first* attempt failed, at least—but he's not one to give up. He failed to deliver the kill and he gave up his identity in the process, so he couldn't join on the cruise. That's why he asked me to do this part of the job. And all of it happened... because of you."

Shafer babbled, "Huh... what? How did I mess up a hit without even knowing?" Then, before Ash could respond, everything fell into place: the Brimley's house, the hit, the vacation. His jaw dropped in stunned understanding.

"You figured it out, didn't you?" Ash grinned down at Shafer. "I can see the look on your face. C'mon, I want to hear you say it."

"The... the car." Shafer barely managed the words as he was trying to believe what he was saying. "Mr. Brimley's car. *He's* the target, and somebody messed with the car. It wasn't an accident. It was supposed to kill him... but he let me take the drive."

Ash nodded with approval. "You have good sense about you, Shafer. I can tell you've grown up around an uncle so involved in the FBI. You're sharp and can piece things together."

It was a lot to take in. "There's still something I don't get. Who was it? Who tampered with the car?"

"You tell me."

Shafer thought back, racking his brain. *If, according to Ash, Klaw had revealed his identity, then Shafer must have seen him, right?* A switch flipped in his brain as he remembered something very specific, and he exclaimed, "The groundsman! The new groundsman... Sylvio?"

"Exactly."

"Stuart didn't remember the man's name at first, and that's because he wasn't expecting Sylvio. He expected somebody else because Sylvio *didn't belong.*"

"I get it, you're clever," Ash said. "But I really don't care how you figured this out."

Shafer quickly shifted topics. "Then tell me something else. Why Stuart? Why is somebody trying to kill him? He's so... I don't know... nice." Mr. Brimley might be absurdly rich, but he also seemed like the kind of person who couldn't upset anybody enough to make mortal enemies.

"Business, I think," Ash answered, once again reaching down from his chair to play in the sand. He pinched a bit of it between three fingers and rubbed it together, raining tiny granules back down to the beach.

"What do you mean?"

"I'm not sure, honestly," Ash admitted. "I don't know who's paying for it. I don't know the reasoning. None of that. But I've been in this game long enough to know that if a man like Brimley is on somebody's hit list, then it's because of his company."

"Like a competitor wants him dead?"

Ash nodded. He seemed bored. "Yeah, that's usually how it works. Sometimes, if you're trying to win the game, it's easier to hurt the other team than to get better yourself, you know?"

"That doesn't seem like good business."

"*Good* business doesn't exist."

Shafer wasn't finished yet. He asked, "Wait, if you're supposed to be killing Stuart, why are you here? Why are you with me?"

"I won't be with you much longer," Ash answered. "But, if you really must know, I've already done my work."

The words twisted Shafer's stomach. "Stuart's... dead? What? I thought—"

"He's not dead... *yet*," Ash answered. "But it's just a matter of time."

Shafer didn't know what to say. He stared back blankly, wrestling with the recurring feeling of confusion.

Ash went on, "From what Klaw told me, one of the most important parts of this hit was making sure it looked accidental. Every move we made was calculated to look like an accident, from the car 'malfunction,' to the carbon monoxide poisoning, to... well... our safety net."

While Ash spoke, Shafer wrestled with the rope binding his hands under the sand. "What do you mean by safety net?"

Ash chuckled. He seemed more interested in the sand around him than the conversation.

"*What* safety net?"

"Just technical problems with the ship." Ash shrugged.

"You're going to kill the engine?"

"Eh, not quite."

"Then what?"

"You ask a lot of questions."

"You're the one who came to talk to *me*," Shafer shot back.

"Fair," admitted Ash. "I suppose you're right, but this is the last thing I'm telling you because I have things to do."

"I'm gonna sunburn before you ever get the words out."

Finally, Ash pointed out toward the ocean. Toward the *Delta Voyager*. "The fuel tank has a problem."

"What kind of problem?"

"A problem that... well..." Ash paused, adjusting his Kevlar vest. "The kind of problem that happens to fuel tanks when a custom explosive is attached to them and set on a countdown timer."

Again, Shafer's jaw dropped and his eyes widened. After a gasp, he asked, "*You're blowing up the Delta Voyager?*"

"I'll be honest, I thought it was an incredibly, um, *direct* approach myself when Klaw first told me, but he's right: it's not only going to be quite effective, but it's also designed to look like one huge, tragic accident, and all of it's going down in just a couple of hours."

"You're going to kill thousands of people just to make money! This is insane!" Shafer was yelling now. He jerked his arms around, doing whatever he could to break loose in the sand, but nothing worked.

"I'm only a little different than the CEO of a fast-food chain," Ash mused. "We're *both* killing lots of people, but I'm going to do it much more quickly. That's the humane way, right?"

"How the hell did you get a bomb on the ship?"

"Same way I got you *off* the ship. If you're wearing a captain's uniform, they don't care what you're bringing on or off. I had no idea. I could have made a career as a sea-faring drug smuggler."

"That's probably better than—"

Ash interrupted, "Seriously. I'm on the clock. Let's move on to the part where I tell you what's about to happen."

"No, wait. I have one more question. Please..."

After biting his lip, looking back over his shoulder to the ocean, and then sighing, Ash said, "What? Let's hear it, but be quick. Last one—and I mean it."

"You aren't allowed to kill me," Shafer said. "But... why? Who wanted me spared? Is that why I'm buried in the sand?"

"To be fair, that was like three questions." Ash snorted as he stood. "Honestly, Shafer, I can't answer that." He picked up the chair, then changed his mind and set it back down.

"Oh c'mon."

"No." He shook his head in objection. "Not because I don't want to tell you, but because I'm not sure. Klaw was insistent on it. He..." Ash hesitated like he was putting great thought into selecting his words. "I think he likes you. You've impressed him."

"I've impressed a hitman?" The sun was getting higher in the sky, but Shafer squinted back at Ash. "I guess that's a good thing."

"Why is that?"

"Because it's keeping me alive."

Ash scrunched his lips to one side of his mouth, examining Shafer for a moment, then said, "I might be overstepping, but I'd say you're in a pretty bad place."

Shafer looked down the beach to his right, then to his left. Settled sand stretched as far as the eye could see in both directions. Unlike the beaches of Grand Turk, there were no signs of life here. Just nature. Just beauty.

"Somebody's going to find me," Shafer said. "I have faith."

Ash looked at the watch strapped to his wrist. It was old-fashioned. The kind without apps. He said, "If somebody is going to find you, Shafer, they better do it quickly."

"What do you mean?"

Ash took a step back, turning to the ocean. By now, the *Delta Voyager* was so far away that it was becoming just a speck on the horizon.

"You're not very ocean-savvy, are you?"

"I mean, I know not to swim too deep. I know to be aware of what's around you."

"Do you know anything about the changing of tides?"

"Yeah. I know the moon's gravity causes the water to rise and fall. I know…" He trailed off as the all-too-familiar feeling of a racing heart fluttered in his chest. "Oh… oh crap."

Ash smirked, giving one more look to his watch. "If somebody is going to find you, they have about eight minutes to do it, because the high tide is coming, Shafer, and soon you'll drown."

"I…" Shafer's stomach dropped. "No. I thought you couldn't kill me? I thought—"

"*I* can't kill you, no," Ash said with another smirk, "But Klaw never said anything about you drowning."

"You're a monster."

Ash ignored him. "I wish I could stick around and see the show, but I have too much to do. Money to collect. Work to admire."

"You won't get away with this."

"Cliché," Ash laughed. "But a very good try. Goodbye, Shafer."

With that, he was gone. The soft crunch of footsteps through the sand tickled Shafer's ear for a moment more, but soon the sound had faded enough that it was masked by the steady wash of the ocean.

The ocean.

Shafer fixed his eyes on the waves and immediately confirmed Ash's words. High tide was coming. Every wave was reaching a bit higher up the beach shore than the previous. Each one, frothy and blue, carried a promise of death.

As he began to writhe in the sand, desperately trying to break loose, a dark thought struck Shafer: Many people would kill for this view. He wasn't that lucky. Instead, this view was going to kill *him*.

FOURTEEN:
EIGHT MINUTES

Shafer squirmed. He jerked and wiggled and shook, side-to-side, up-and-down, and twisting every direction. He fought and pushed for what felt like ages, but in the end, he made no progress. Not only was he still buried, but he was also panting, winded.

When he managed to dislodge any of the sand, his next move shook more back in the same place. It was an endless loop and he was getting nowhere.

The rise of the water, however, was unhampered. The waves continued reaching closer and closer to him. Beaches were supposed to be relaxing. Peaceful. Instead, all he could think about was drowning.

The mist of the ocean became a constant spray to his face. Unable to wipe his eyes, he squinted them shut. The salty water irritated and burned anyway. There was no escaping it.

Shafer moved on to his next approach.

"Help!" He yelled out. "Help me!"

No response.

"Please! Somebody, help!" Shouting took a lot of air, which was hard to come by with the sand pressed against his chest. Giving up, he took in as deep a breath as he could, inhaling the seaspray as well. His mouth tasted of salt.

"This is just sand," he grumbled. "How is it this hard to move in *sand?*"

A wave washed even closer, up to the back legs of the old lawn chair. His time was running low. If he was going to get out of here, he had to think. He needed a plan, and he needed it now.

He tried flexing. The subtle swelling of both his arms and legs pressed into the sand, pushing it away from him. When he relaxed, he didn't lose ground. The sand held its place, and he had a little more room to work.

He took a deep breath, pushing out his chest as far as the sand allowed, and then he forced it out even further, pushing more sand away. Once again, as he relaxed, the sand held its place.

This was it. If he was going to get out of here, it wasn't going to be by thrashing around madly. No, if he wanted to escape, it had to be *slowly*. Bit by bit. Methodical moves.

But did he have the time? The biggest waves were coming in only feet away. They'd reached the front legs of the lawn chair.

Shafer stuck out his jaw and began carving the sand away from his neck. Soon, he'd gained enough ground that he could extend his head forward, but it didn't help him much. If anything, he could only reach closer toward the ocean.

"Okay, new approach," Shafer said as he began to work on freeing his hands. If he could get them free, it might just save his life.

He started small, with only his thumbs. Moving them up and down, he burrowed out the sand around them. The waves were only a couple of feet from his face.

Shafer squinted again as beads of water ran down his face. His hair was soaked and water dripped from it, down to his cheeks.

"C'mon, Shafer. You can do this."

He was making progress, but it was very, very slow. The water was coming too quickly, the tide was rising too high, and the harsh reality was setting in: Shafer was going to drown, and the Brimley's, along with the rest of the passengers aboard the *Delta Voyager,* would soon be killed in an explosion.

Even as the first wave slapped Shafer's chin, he kept working but also knew it wasn't going to be enough. With his fingers clasped together, he'd carved out a decent amount of space for them to move, but his arms were still mostly locked in place.

Desperately, he tried extending his feet like he was standing on his tiptoes, but as he pushed down on the sand, his body rose and the sudden shift collapsed sand into the rest of the space he'd freed. In one fatal move, he'd lost every bit of what he'd slowly gained.

He nearly swore but had to force his mouth closed as the water slapped him in the face. Squinting, he leaned his head back, breathing in a long breath of air, knowing not how many he had left.

Crash!

The sound startled him to the point that he jolted before trying to figure out what had happened.

It was the chair. The waves had overturned it, and it fell so close that it had nearly struck him in the head.

To an extent, the chair did shield Shafer from the brunt of the waves, but the tide was still rising and water still wrapped around his neck.

"What can I do?" He desperately looked around, searching for any answer. *Was this it? He was going to die on vacation because he couldn't leave well enough alone?* Yes, he'd saved May and her family the first time, but now *everybody* was going to die and Shafer was about to drown.

The worst part was that May was right—this was *his* fault. He was here because he couldn't leave well enough alone.

But he cared. He cared about her so much, and as the water rose to the bottom of his chin, he knew that even if he was going to die, he wasn't going down without a fight. He would try *something*. He had to. For himself. For May and her parents. For all the passengers.

He pictured the smug look on Ash's face as he checked his watch, as he'd bid Shafer farewell. He pictured the man strolling away, headed to God-knew-where to contact somebody about God-knew-what.

Ash couldn't win. This Klaw person—whoever he was—couldn't win. Or, at least, if they *were* going to win and if Shafer was going to drown, he wasn't going to do it without first exhausting every last idea.

And that's why he leaned forward and sank his teeth into the leg of the chair. It was impulsive. It was a long shot. But it was also the only thing he hadn't tried. Trying to push his way *up* through the sand was getting him nowhere, but maybe he could lift himself by using the chair to press *down*.

His teeth clamped onto the chair's leg with so much force that he was worried it might break. Another wave rolled in, thrashing Shafer in the face, but he didn't let go. Jaw clamped, he lowered his chin and planted the chair in the sand.

With a grunt, Shafer felt his entire core tightening. His abdominal muscles strained and his neck felt curled, but he pushed down with the chair using all his strength. It sank a couple of inches, swirling sand through the water, but then it caught and no longer continued to sink.

Instead, Shafer started to rise.

It was only inches, but it was a start. He relaxed for a moment, assessing his possession. His shoulders had emerged from the sand, but he only glimpsed them for a moment before another wave hit and they were once again submerged.

"Getting closer," he encouraged himself through a mouthful of the chair.

As Shafer positioned for another go at it, he took a deep breath, but just as he was breathing in, a huge wave of water bombarded him and he inhaled a big gulp of it.

Coughing ensued. Major coughing. He choked and gasped, trying to fight back the water he'd accidentally swallowed. It was all he could do to hang onto the chair.

Once he recovered, while also timing the incoming waves in his head, he worked the chair back as he'd had it, let a wave roll past, and made his next attempt as soon as he was clear.

This time, as he used the chair to hoist himself

through the sand, he added a twist. He shimmied with his shoulders, rocking back and forth as his entire body, oxygen-depleted and exhausted, fought against him.

It worked. First, his shoulder shook free, and soon his chest followed. Keeping the chair in his mouth, he repositioned, reaching forward and burying it into the sand once again, then repeating. Soon his elbows appeared. His hips. Then his hands, which were bound together with a thin brown rope.

Shafer let go of the chain, and with his hands out, he dug his elbows into the sand and crawled loose. As he climbed out of his could-have-been sandy tomb, a big wave washed over it, flooding it all together.

He was free.

As Shafer clambered to his feet, he let out a big sigh. Panting, he picked up the chair as it floated past. "You saved my life," he told it. "Thanks."

It didn't respond, but Shafer didn't have time to carry on a conversation either way. He had bigger issues at hand.

Turning back to the ocean, the *Delta Voyager* was the tiniest of dots by now. *What could he do?* He headed down the beach, heading toward the only possible escape he'd seen: the motorboat.

When he'd first spotted it, it had barely been floating in the way. By now the water had risen high enough the boat was pulling against its rope.

Shafer's focus shifted to getting his hands unbound. The knot was simple, and he guessed he could untie it with his teeth. After a minute of work and a mouth full of gritty sand, he proved himself right: the rope came loose and he unwound it from his wrists, shaking his hands to get more blood flowing to them.

"Much better." He was free, but still in rough shape. His clothes were soaked and muddy. He was covered with sand, which clung to both his clothes and skin. He could feel it all over his body, refusing to let go.

But he had survived. He was alive, and he had to do something to make sure everybody aboard the *Delta Voyager* stayed that way, too.

The motorboat, on closer inspection, wasn't in the best shape. As he reached it, he asked it, "What are you doing here? Do you work?"

Climbing into the rusty vessel, Shafer took a seat on the cracked leather bench seat that looked like it had seen more than its fair share of time underneath a tropical sun. The motor was in the back, but the ignition was in front of the seat. To his amazement, he found the key in the ignition.

"Oh, that's too easy." Suspicious of his good fortune, he turned his eyes to the gauges and peered through the foggy glass to see that the fuel tank was nearly full.

This boat was prepared to leave, and it couldn't have been a coincidence. He didn't know who had left it or where it was supposed to go, but it was ready to go at a moment's notice. A getaway—about to become *Shafer's* getaway.

He'd gone boating quite a few times in rentals with his uncle, but those boats were a little different. They were more modern and complicated, with fancy buttons and levers, knobs to twist, and gears to turn. This one had an ignition switch, a steering wheel, a throttle, and a motor. That was all.

But that was all he needed.

Holding his breath, Shafer grabbed the key. He twisted it.

Nothing.

And then, after a painful second of silence, there was a hum underneath his feet. The boat vibrated and the engine roared to life.

He looked around. "All right, now what?"

The boat was still tied down, so he jumped out, splashing down to the ocean below, and grabbed the anchor, feverishly untying it. Every second he wasted here was a second less he'd have to get everybody off the *Delta Voyager*.

As the rope came untied, the boat began to float, and since Shafer wasn't sure how to put the motor in reverse, he did the next best thing, manually pulling the boat around in the water while the motor continued to hum. He pointed it out to sea, in the direction of the *Delta Voyager*.

With a solid heading, he climbed back up into the boat with a soft grin on his face. This was going well—or as well as he could hope, at least.

Then he heard the shouting. "Damn you, Shafer!"

"Ah, crap." As the boat motored forward, Shafer spun around to see a figure running onto the beach, waving his hands and shouting. It was Szalay. Or Ash. Or whoever. The man of many names had returned, and he didn't look happy.

"Come back here," Ash yelled, sprinting toward the ocean.

Shafer wasted no time pushing the throttle forward. As the boat lurched forward, he yelled, "You said you didn't have time to watch me not-drown!"

DELTA ADRIFT

Ash responded by drawing a pistol and cracking three shots at Shafer, who immediately threw himself to the floor of the boat.

"Come back!" Ash bellowed. "I'm not done with you." Two more shots were fired, both of which slammed into the boat but missed Shafer.

Shafer didn't respond. He was too busy trying to stay in the boat as it sped forward so fast that it skipped across the waves.

As he peeped over the seat, Shafer saw Ash lower his gun and head back to the trees on the far side of the beach, moving at a dead sprint. He was going somewhere, and he was doing so with a purpose.

"I swear, if he has another boat..." Shafer trailed off as he realized something that didn't add up. His knee was wet. And not wet from his clothes—a constant wet. Standing water.

He looked down and understood: A shallow pool of water filled the bottom of the boat.

"What the..." Before he could finish his sentence, he spotted the problem. Water was spilling into the boat, coming from two bullet holes in the side paneling.

"Of course." He quickly tried to cover up the holes with one hand while reaching to the steering wheel with his other. Despite his best efforts, water continued to seep into the boat, and soon it was covering the entire floor. One way or another, his boat was sinking.

Shafer turned his eyes to the horizon, peering out across the ocean and scanning for the *Delta Voyager*. Had he lost itt? Was it out of sight? If so, all hope was lost.

Just when he was feeling overcome with dread, the *Delta Voyager* came into focus in the very distant morning light. It was sailing east, toward the rising sun, and hope stirred inside Shafer.

Maybe it wasn't too late. If he could get to the ship, maybe they'd have time to get everybody off. Maybe everybody could be saved.

But there were a lot of maybe's—too many for comfort—and that wasn't even considering the biggest question of all. As more water trickled into the bottom of his tiny boat, he couldn't help but wonder if he'd even make it to the *Delta Voyager,* or if he'd drown before he could ever get there.

FIFTEEN:
ALL HANDS ON DECK

Shafer was ankle-deep in water by the time he steered his motorboat beside the *Delta Voyager*. To make matters worse, the enormous cruise ship churned the ocean so that the wake violently bounced the small motorboat, making it a struggle to go straight.

"Hey!" he shouted. "Hey!" With a jostle, his boat slammed into the side of the ship, and for a split second, he was afraid he'd be thrown out and sucked underwater.

Instead, he regained his balance and peered through a porthole beside him. He was looking into a passenger's room. If he could get somebody's attention, then they could flag for help.

Pounding his fists on the window, he shouted, "Anybody in there? Hello?"

No response came. The room's television was on but the occupants had left. His boat sputtered.

As he began losing hope, a shout came from above. "Hey! You, down there!"

Shafer spotted a sunglass-wearing man in his late thirties hanging over the railing of the fifth deck. "Hey man!" he yelled back. "I could really use some help!"

"What's going on? Are you trying to…" The man trailed off, suddenly overcome by a look of recognition. "Wait a minute, you're the boy who saved all those people. You're… Shafer. It's Shafer, right?"

Shafer's boat lurched, taking on even more water. He could feel it sinking. Waves were jumping over the sides as the motor tried to carry on.

"Yeah," he replied. "That's me. And I'm trying to save some more people, but I need help."

"What can I do?"

"I'm sinking." Shafer cautiously stood, but the sudden movement caused him to slip, falling backward and nearly out of the boat. He cursed.

"Gimme a sec," the man shouted down to him before disappearing over the railing.

Shafer gritted his teeth as he watched the man go. "I'm afraid that's about all the time I have left." His engine sputtered and coughed. Time was running out.

And then, just when Shafer was sure he was about to go down, he heard a yell from the fifth deck. "Catch!" A life preserver came flying over the side of the ship.

Not a second after he grabbed onto it, Shafer's boat gave one final shutter and the engine died. With a gurgle, the ocean took it away, pulling it under the *Delta Voyager* and out of sight.

Shafer clutched onto the preserver and the thick white rope tied around him as it pulled him through the water. Behind him, a metal *crunch* came as the small motorboat was shredded on the hull of the cruise ship. He let out a weak laugh. "Yikes. That... that could have been me."

"Put that ring on and I'll pull you up," the man called down.

"You can do that?"

"I was heading to the gym, but hey, this can be my workout instead."

Following instructions, Shafer looped the life preserver around his body, then said, "I'm good!"

"Hold on!"

Almost immediately, Shafer felt his body begin to rise. He'd ascend for a moment, pause, then rise some more. Once his body was completely out of the water, he put his soggy shoes on the hull of the ship and began climbing up the rope.

He yelled, "If you can hold the rope, I can help do some of the work."

A strained "*thanks*" came from overhead.

Shafer made good on his promise, and soon he was being helped over the railing by the astonished stranger, who looked over Shafer's clothes, shoes, and overall condition before asking, "What happened, man? You look rough."

Shafer was panting by now. "It's been a wild night. But listen, you need to go to your room and get ready to evacuate the ship."

The man's expression changed from astonished to confused. "Wait, what?"

"You need to get ready to evacuate," Shafer repeated. "And tell your neighbors. Tell everybody in the hall. I need to go find Captain Graf."

"Are you serious? What do you mean? What's wrong?" The man was spouting off questions faster than Shafer could even process them all.

Shafer lowered his voice. "I can't explain right now, but trust me. We've got to do this."

The man's face had turned whiter than the sunscreen streaking his cheeks. "This is… this is nuts."

Shafer nodded. "I know. But you gotta trust me."

Slowly the man nodded, then with a look of determination, he turned and hurried away. Shafer watched him disappear through two sliding doors, then sighed. *Was this just normal life for him now?*

He didn't have time to come up with an answer. He had to find Graf, but he had to do something else *first*.

He set off in a hurry, heading toward the Brimley's room. He knew that if Graf sounded the alarm, the ship would be pure chaos. The Brimley's would be looking for Shafer, and he was sure that they wouldn't get off the ship until they found him. They'd go down with the ship.

Shafer hadn't been aboard the *Delta Voyager* long enough to see all of the ship, so he quickly got the self-guided tour as he ran through an arcade and a casino while drawing looks from the people he encountered.

In the end, he never made it to the Brimley's suite. Instead, once he reached the ninth deck, he rounded a corner to come face-to-face with a very worried May.

The worry on her face, however, quickly transitioned to annoyance as she recognized him. "Shafer, what the hell have you been doing?" she asked. "I went into your room and your phone was there, and…" Her eyes widened when she got a better look at him. "What happened to you?"

"You remember that part of a conversation when you said I go out and look for danger?"

"Yes." The words shot out of her mouth.

"Yeah, so... Actually, where are your parents?"

"In the room. We were getting ready for breakfast, but I thought you might be in the gym. I was worried though because it's later and..."

"I need to talk to them. And you. Everybody. *Now*."

Wasting no time, Shafer took May by the hand and pulled her along. "C'mon. This is important."

"You're scaring me, Shafe."

"I'm sorry. Just come here."

Mr. and Mrs. Brimley, both dressed in their best beast-vacation wear, were leaving their room as Shafer and May approached.

Mrs. Brimley spotted him first, then did a double-take on his appearance. "Shafer? Honey, what happened? Why are you muddy?"

Shafer lowered his voice. "I know I'm going to sound completely crazy, but you've got to believe everything I'm about to say."

They both looked concerned. Mr. Brimley said, "Of course, Shafer. Is something wrong?"

"*Lots* of things are wrong," Shafer answered, then lowered his voice even more. "Somebody is trying to kill you, Stuart."

Mrs. Brimley and May both gasped.

Mr. Brimley raised both of his eyebrows, and after a moment of confusion, he asked, "What? Why? Who? Shafer, how do you know this?"

Shafer quickly answered, "Lemme summarize. Last

night, Captain Szalay was acting suspicious, so I followed him into this hallway that runs beside our room that has all the vents and pipes and stuff. He had this device that emits some sort of poison vapor, apparently, and he was flooding it into your room through the ducts, but I fought him and broke the device."

May and her parents all stared back in astonishment.

Shafer went on. "So he fought back and knocked me out, and while I was out, he smuggled me off the boat, and when I awoke, I was buried in sand up to my neck on a nearby beach. That's when he told me about his plans to kill you, Stuart."

There was more silence, until finally, an astonished Mr. Brimley asked, "So, why does the assistant captain want me dead?"

"Sorry, I left that out," Shafer apologized. "Szalay isn't a captain-in-training. He's a hitman named Ash, and he's working with another hitman, who's working for some businessperson who wants you dead."

Mr. Brimley rubbed his brow, deep in thought. "Shafer, did you get a name?"

"Of the businessman?" He shook his head. "No. We didn't talk for too long, and then Ash left, and the rising tide was supposed to come in and drown me."

May, with trembling lips, asked, "How did you escape?"

"Um…" Shafer knew they didn't have much time. "I'll tell you later, I promise. But we've got to get you off the boat, Stuart."

Finally, Mrs. Brimley spoke up. "If they're after Stu, can we just stay in our room and get some security around here?"

Mr. Brimley shook his head. "I'm not sure that the cruise ship has enough security, love." Despite the grimness of the situation, his words were almost playful.

Shafer had to rain down even more bad news. "That's where the problem comes in. They've exhausted two attempts to kill you, so the third plan is supposedly fool-proof."

"What's the third plan?" Mr. Brimley asked, sounding much more serious.

"Wait, *third* attempt?" Mrs. Brimley backtracked. "What was the other?"

Talking as fast as he could, Shafer answered her first. "It turns out Stuart's car didn't malfunction. It had been manipulated to kill him—I just ended up behind the wheel."

Mrs. Brimley gasped, covering her mouth with a hand.

Shafer then turned to Mr. Brimley. "The third plan is go-big-or-go-home. Ash attached an explosive device to the fuel tank, and it's supposed to blow up the entire ship."

Again, their eyes widened.

Mrs. Brimley stammered, "Shafer, if this was coming from *anybody* else, I'd never believe it."

Shafer nodded. "Yeah, I get that. But this kinda just seems like an average Tuesday at this point."

May put her arms around her father like she was trying to protect him. "What do we do?" Her voice was more solid than Shafer had expected.

"We get everybody off the ship," Shafer replied. "Ash said we only had a couple of hours, and that was probably almost an hour ago. We have to *move*."

Mr. Brimley asked, "What are you thinking, Shafer?"

"I'm thinking I'll get ahold of Captain Graf and tell him to make an announcement, and while I'm doing that, you guys start going door-to-door. Tell everybody to prepare for evacuation."

Mr. Brimley nodded.

Mrs. Brimley, despite shedding a few tears, nodded, too.

May asked, "Shafe, do you still have Graf's phone number?"

"In my room." He looked to the Brimley's and offered the best encouragement he could. "I know this is scary, but we've defied a lot of odds by getting Stuart to this point alive—and we didn't even know. Imagine what we can do when we're actually trying."

"*You've* defied a lot of odds, Shafer," Mr. Brimley pointed out.

"The point is, you're here. Let's keep the ball rolling, keep Stuart alive, and save everybody else." Shafer turned toward his room, but paused. "When they sound the alarm, it's gonna get chaotic, so don't wait for me, no matter what. Go to the lifeboats. I'll come too, but you all need to get off the ship. I can take care of myself."

"We're not leaving without you," Mrs. Brimley said. "What kind of people would we be?"

"No, you *must*," he insisted. "Please. I'll be right behind you, I promise. I can take care of myself."

She didn't agree, but she also didn't object, which Shafer took as reluctant compliance. Forcing a smile, he said, "See you guys on the other side."

*****

"Hello?" The voice crackled through the phone.

"Captain Graf. It's Shafer McCartney."

"Shafer!" Graf sounded chipper. "How are you today? Can I do something for you?"

Shafer dove right in. "Um, yeah. And this is going to sound crazy, but you've gotta believe me."

"Let's hear it."

With no delay, Shafer began to explain everything, making sure to emphasize that the "captain-in-training" was not the person he appeared to be, and that, most importantly, there was a bomb on the ship.

As soon as he'd finished, the only immediate response was silence. He waited for just a moment before prompting, "Um... captain?"

"Holy heart of the sea," Graf's response finally came. "That's... Shafer, are you sure?"

"I'm dead certain," he insisted.

"Shafer, if I sound the alarm and you're wrong... it's *my* ass. My job. I'll lose everything."

Shafer bit his lip, asking himself if there was any way he could be wrong, if Ash could have lied to him. Then, going with his gut, he answered, "Captain, you can trust me. I wouldn't make this up."

Another long pause came. Then, a sigh. "I know. But Shafer, if this was coming from anybody else, I wouldn't believe you."

"Funny enough, I just heard the same thing."

"You're a very unusual boy," Graf said. His breathing was shallow and he was talking fast—he was scared.

Shafer offered his best encouragement. "Captain, it's okay. This is gonna work out. You're a great captain and you're trained for a crisis. You've got this, and I'll do anything I can to help."

"Shafer, thank you…" A long exhalation came through the phone, then a plan. "I'm going to sound the alarm, and the passengers will start filing to the evacuation zones. How much time do we have?"

"I'd think an hour at most, maybe?"

"We can get everybody off." Graf sounded surprisingly confident. "Meanwhile, I'm going to radio for help. I'll get some nearby ships heading this way, and then… well… then I'm going down to the fuel room to look for the bomb."

This caught Shafer by surprise. "Captain Graf… what? You don't know how to diffuse it, do you?"

"No. Not the slightest idea."

"Then why look for it?"

There was a pause, then an uncertain answer. "Um… If it isn't attached to anything, we can throw it over the deck. If we could get in the water, we could save the ship. We could save *everything*."

Shafer couldn't keep the slight grin off his face. "Captain, I like the way you think." After a second of debate, he added, "I'm coming with you."

"Shafer, no! I'm sorry, but I can't let you do that."

"Listen," he immediately argued. "This, sadly, isn't the first time I've been face-to-face with a bomb. I've been through this once, and you might need help."

After one more pause, Graf reluctantly agreed. "Fine. Meet me outside my quarters in five minutes."

"Count on it."

"Shafer?"

"Yes?"

"Let's go save a cruise ship."

SIXTEEN:
TICKING AWAY

Shafer didn't tell May what he was doing. In part, it was because he hadn't seen her again. Mostly, though, it was because he knew what she'd say.

But in the end, he was doing what he knew was best.

And that's why, when Captain Graf stepped out of his office and gave Shafer a nod, Shafer knew he'd made the right decision.

The *Delta Voyager* had been in utter chaos since the evacuation announcement. There had been yelling, shouting, and mass pandemonium while a siren and announcement looped over the loudspeakers: "Passengers, please prepare for evacuation. Make your way to your assigned evacuation station. This is not a drill."

Despite the safety meeting, everybody seemed unprepared. They were scurrying around, wildly yelling at each other. Some were in pajamas, some in swimsuits, and one man was even wearing a robe.

The crewmembers were barking instructions: "This way, people. Move!"

"Sir, put that bag down! No personal items aboard the lifeboats."

"Scoot in closer, we've got to fit more people on this deck."

Complete havoc had broken loose.

And the man who had triggered it all looked impressively composed as he exited the captain's quarters. "Shafer," he greeted.

"Captain Graf."

"Are you sure about this? You don't have to join me."

"I'm positive. I told the Brimley's not to wait on me, and they're my biggest concern."

Graf almost let out a laugh. "Always looking out for everybody else."

"Nah, I just know they wouldn't evacuate if they were looking for me."

"I understand that," Graf said. "I've filled my first mate in on what's happening, so he's leading the evacuation for now. Let's do this."

Shafer gestured to the stairs. "Lead the way, Captain."

They headed across the deck. Graf called out to a crew member, "Celia, I think station five is understaffed. Go downstairs, help where you can, and then board up. Stay safe."

"Yes, Captain," she answered back. Her voice quivered like she was scared but was also reluctant to admit it to herself. "What's wrong? Why are we evacuating?"

Graff bit his lip for just a moment, thinking as he

kept his stride. "It's very well nothing," he lied. "But there might be some technical problems with the engine and this is a precaution."

The woman nodded, suddenly looking more sure of herself. "Thanks, Captain. Best of luck."

They kept on, and Graf took Shafer down a different set of stairs toward the back of the boat, joking, "I hope you're in better shape than me, Shafer."

"We got a lot of stairs to do, huh?"

"Just eleven flights now."

"I'm about to regret all those trips to the buffet, I just know it."

Graff cackled. "You're good at this."

"At what?"

"At... I don't know. Saving the world."

"I wouldn't say this is exactly 'the world,' but thanks."

As they rounded another flight of stairs, Graf said, "I mean it, and it's a good trait to have. You calmed me down, and I really didn't know how I was going to get through this when you first told me what was happening. You just have something about you... the way you deal with adversity."

"Sadly, that comes from experience," Shafer replied. "But don't sell yourself short. I was watching you with that lady upstairs. You did exactly for her what you're saying I did for you. She was scared, and you helped."

"By lying to the poor girl," Graff said back, suddenly whispering.

"That's not entirely what happened," Shafer argued. "Sometimes it's better to say what people need to hear than what they should hear. As long as she gets off the boat, all is well, and now she's a lot more relaxed, which will only help calm down the passengers around her. You did good, Captain Graf."

"Thanks, Shafer. That really means a lot."

They pressed on in silence. After about seven flights of stairs, Shafer was growing tired, and Graf was in even worse shape. He was panting to catch his breath, but also only stopping to occasionally redirect a worried passenger desperately looking for the evacuation zones.

As they reached the third deck, Graf said, "It might not be the time to ask, but I don't understand something, Shafer."

"What's that?"

"Why the boat? Why is somebody trying to blow up my ship? Is this terrorism?"

At the words, Shafer realized he'd never told the captain the rest of the story—too much had been on his mind. He quickly recounted everything he knew: the hit on Mr. Brimley, the identity of 'Captain Szalay', and even the attempted poisoning of the Brimley's from the previous night.

Finally, they arrived at the first deck. Graf headed down the hall, shaking his head. "All this was going on under my nose? That's unbelievable."

"Hey, don't feel bad about that," Shafer consoled. "The only way I knew about it is because I couldn't sleep last night and happened to see Szalay sneaking around the hallway and followed him. What are the odds of that?"

"Very slim?"

"Exactly. And very lucky. If I wouldn't have seen him, then May and her family, well…" Shafer trailed off. They both knew how that story would have ended.

At the end of the hall was a wide door with a sign

that read, *Crew Members Only*. By the time they reached it, Graf had a key in hand. He unlocked it and pushed it open. "Welcome to the crew quarters."

Shafer glanced at the sign on the door and pointed out, "Last time I snuck past one of these signs, I woke up buried on a beach."

"You... wait? What?"

Shafer shook his head. "Never mind, shouldn't have gone there." He forced a laugh. "I'll tell you about it when we're safe and sound, okay?"

"You better. Sounds like I was out of the loop on *a lot* of stuff."

"You're running a big-ass boat. You can't know everything that happens on it. Or off it. Or... whatever. Let's just find this bomb."

They descended another flight of stairs, entering the crew quarters.

Ultimately, it was disappointing. Even on the lower passenger decks of the ship, there was an attempt at being clean and elegant. Under the boat, however, the rooms were smaller, the hallways were more narrow, and the carpet was a drab grey.

Graf continued down the hall, unlocking a second door. "Down here," he panted.

As soon as Shafer stepped through the second doorway, it was loud. Very loud. And it was hot, too. More noises than he could ever identify hit him all at once: the whistle of steam, the roar of engines, and the rush of hydraulic pistons, among others.

The volume was so great that Graf had to shout. "This is the engine room."

"I see that." Shafer ran his eyes along the room,

taking in the enormous engine and its many parts. "This thing is crazy!"

"Parts of it are really hot, too," Graf said, and on cue, a jet of steam burst out of a valve. "Don't touch anything, especially since you haven't been trained. The steam alone would melt your face off."

"Geez. Yeah, thanks for the heads-up."

"Follow me."

They journeyed through the room, snaking past the various offshoots of the tremendous engine. Soon, they had made it to the far side, arriving at another door labeled with a *no smoking beyond this point* sign.

Graf shouted, "This is the fuel room."

Pointing to the sign, Shafer joked, "Hey, does this mean you can smoke in the engine room?"

Graf shook his head, grinning. "No, actually."

"Can you smoke on the boat?"

"No."

"Then why is this sign here?"

Graf shrugged before answering. "I'll make you a deal. You help me save this boat, and I'll let you take it down."

"Now we're talking," Shafer replied. "Let's go."

They slipped through the door, not even bothering to take the time to close it.

"Wow…" Shafer said, taking in the next room.

It was long. Very long, stretching back almost as far as he could see. In the middle of the room were two enormous tanks, side by side. Each of them was about three feet taller than Shafer, and he guessed they were about 60 feet long. Pipes led from them to the engine room.

"That's so much fuel," he said.

"It's a big ship, my friend," Graf replied. "You said the explosive was with the fuel tanks?"

"That's what Ash told me."

"Ash… like Captain Szalay?"

"That's the one."

"Then let's look for this bomb."

They made their way across the room, approaching the fuel tanks cautiously, with their eyes peeled for anything out of the ordinary. Graf asked, "Any idea what we should be looking for, exactly?"

Shafer shook his head. "Your guess is as good as mine."

"What did the last bomb you saw look like?"

He thought back. "Well, it was huge and shiny. But, I mean, it was also a nuke, so this is probably a little different. It wouldn't take much to spark the fuel tanks."

"You're right about that," Graf said grimly. "And with the amount of fuel we have now, I…" He suddenly gasped and said, "Shafer! Look!"

Shafer followed his gaze, expecting to see the explosive, but that wasn't the case. Instead, he spotted something else.

A person. Lying face down in a pool of blood was one of the ship's crew members, wearing an unmistakable blue uniform. Shafer didn't see the man's face, but he didn't need to. He already knew. The man was dead.

"That's…" Graf said. "That's Ramirez. He must have come down for the hourly inspection and stumbled upon the bomb being planted, but that means…"

Both Shafer and Graf turned back to the fuel tanks, and they both fell dead silent as their eyes fell upon the item for which they were searching.

It was small, about the size of a tissue box. Most of the exterior was a shiny metal, but the bottom half contained a vial of clear liquid. Two wires led from the vial to the rest of the frame, and a small screen glowed on it, much like a digital clock. Shafer leaned forward, peering at the tiny red numbers: *41:13*.

The numbers ticked down. They had less than an hour before the bomb detonated.

Both Shafer and Graf froze upon seeing it, but Shafer came out of the trance a little more quickly. He walked over to the bomb, careful not to step in the pool of sticky blood. "This... this isn't what I was expecting," he said, carefully looking over the handcrafted explosive.

Graf followed behind him, his breathing becoming raspy. "Why is that? It's exactly what you said it would be."

"Yeah, I know." Shafer stood in silence for a moment, examining the explosive more closely, trying to take everything in. Something was off. He didn't know what it was, but he could tell. Something was wrong.

"How's it attached?" Graf asked, approaching the bomb like it was a poisonous snake ready to strike. "Is that... duct tape?"

He was right. The bomb was taped to the tank with strips of duct tape on all four sides. "Yeah actually," Shafer confirmed. "Ash really went all-out with the delivery."

"What do we do with it?" Graf had made it beside Shafer, leaning over to look at the wires. "I really don't know anything about explosives."

"I wish Stuart were here," Shafer mumbled.

"He knows explosives?"

"He knows *everything*. I swear he's read every book,

ever. He might not have studied explosives officially, but he would be more qualified than me, I'm sure."

Graf asked, "Should we go get him?"

For a moment, Shafer contemplated this. "I... I think..." He changed his mind mid-sentence. "No, I don't think so. Hopefully, he's already evacuated by now. We can handle this."

"So what should we do with it?" Graf asked. "Do you think we could unfasten it and carry it upstairs? If we could throw it into the ocean, that would save us from the blast."

Slowly, Shafer nodded. "That sounds like a good option, and if we do it, we need to attach the bomb to something heavy so it sinks." He sighed, taking in the makeshift nature of the explosive, then cautioned, "But I'm not sure about transporting it. What it if detonates while we're carrying it?"

"Wasn't it carried down here to start with?" Graf asked.

"Yeah, it was. But it was probably armed once it was put in place," Shafer countered.

"See, you do know a little about explosives."

Shafer shrugged. "I guess you have to when your uncle leads the FBI."

"I wish *he* were here right now."

"You and I both, Captain."

Once again, Graf asked, "So then what do you think we should do?"

As Shafer looked over the explosive one more time, he said, "I think we have three options: We can try to throw it overboard, cut one of the wires and try to diffuse it, or we can let it explode and take down the boat, but have all the passengers evacuated. The last option is the safest because it's the only one where we're not messing with the bomb. It's the only one where we're sure nobody dies."

After some contemplative silence, Graf said, "Shafer... I'm not sure that's the case."

The way Graf spoke made Shafer's heart sink. Reluctantly, he asked, "What do you mean?"

Graf pointed to the timer, which now read *37:51*. "Time is the issue," he said. "The evacuation procedure is designed to take slightly less time than how long the boat should take to sink, but *explosions* aren't calculated into the evacuation plan."

"I thought you said we had enough time?"

"You said a little over an hour. Our timing was a bit off."

Shafer ran the numbers in his head and came to a painful realization. "So by the time this explodes, there will still be people on the ship?"

Slowly, Graf nodded. "I'm afraid so."

"How many people would be left?"

"Best guess? About twenty percent."

The answer snatched the air out of Shafer's lungs. All along, he figured worst-case scenario, they could all evacuate and be safe. That was no longer the case. If he and Graf didn't do something with the bomb, then several hundred people might be killed.

He wasn't ready to risk their lives.

He couldn't.

A knot wound in his stomach until he had another thought. "Wait, didn't you say you had help coming? Who did you reach out to?"

"My immediate responders were three ships and a helicopter."

"A helicopter? Out here?"

"Yeah. I don't know why a helicopter should even be in the area, but I'm not turning down *any* help at this point."

"Makes sense. Do you think we have time to wait for them to arrive?"

Before a response could come, the hair on the back of Shafer's neck stood up. Something was wrong. He could feel it.

That's when he detected movement out of the corner of his eye. Spinning to his left, he spied a figure slipping through the cracked door of the engine room.

It was Ash.

Somehow, the hitman had followed them. Water was dripping off his bulletproof vest and his black eye looked even worse, but he was here. He was *angry*.

As he entered the room, he wore a cold look on his face and had a pistol clutched in his hand. He raised the gun.

Shafer yelled, "Captain Graf, move!" His words didn't come quickly enough.

Bang! The gunshot echoed in the fuel room.

Shafer's ears rang but was unharmed. Ash had missed him.

Captain Graf, however, wasn't as lucky.

SEVENTEEN: THE BATTLE IN THE BOWELS

Graf stumbled. He took two steps backward, fighting to keep his balance as a bloodstain blossomed across the chest of his white captain's uniform. He lifted one hand, reaching out to Shafer with pleading eyes, but it was too late.

"Captain," Shafer yelled. "No… no!"

Graf opened his mouth to speak, and his tongue quivered as it tried to form words, but no words came. Instead, he fell backward, collapsing on the floor with a thud.

Shafer spun to face Ash, who took two more steps into the room, pistol raised. "Shafer, good to see you again," he said.

Shafer looked past the barrel of the pistol to Ash's bruised face. "How'd you get on the boat?"

"Same way as you, I suppose." From the way he said the words, Shafer could tell that Ash was enjoying this.

Shafer slowly pointed to the bomb strapped to the fuel tank beside him. "This doesn't make sense. Your work is done. Why'd you come back to the boat when it's supposed to explode in…" He checked the timer. "…Thirty-six minutes?"

Ash looked at the bomb, then checked his watch for just a second, never lowering the pistol. "When I saw you fleeing the island in my boat, I knew exactly what you were going to do. You were coming here and trying to save the day again because you can't ever just stay out of the way. You wanted to—once again—mess up the job."

"I wanted to save my friends and all the innocent people," Shafer replied. "It's not like I'm targeting you— just trying to protect the rest."

"What a hero."

"The people's champ?"

Ash rolled his eyes but also offered the slightest of smirks. "I knew I had to get to the *Delta Voyager* before you found the bomb, and I know you have narrowed down your three options: try to remove it, try to diffuse it, or try to help get as many evacuated as you can."

"Damn, you're good."

Ash snorted. "Nah, I was just listening through the door for a minute."

"Oh…" Shafer was fresh out of ideas, but he knew he needed to keep Ash talking instead of shooting. "So you came here to prevent me from stopping the explosion?"

"To stop you from *trying* to stop the explosion," Ash corrected. "I couldn't risk this going wrong. Plus, at this point, I don't care what Klaw said. I really want to kill you, Shafer."

"Sweet." Shafer quickly glanced around the room, trying to spot anything he could use to fight back. There was nothing. Absolutely nothing. An explosive, two dead bodies, and lots of fuel.

But maybe that was enough. Suddenly, he had an idea.

Before Ash could speak again, Shafer leaped to his right. Ash followed him with the pistol, arching an eyebrow when Shafer froze in place. "What... what the hell was that?"

Shafer looked down to his feet, then to the fuel tank right behind him. "You shoot me now and the bullet will go right through me and into the fuel tank. One spark, and this whole ship goes up in flames. I die, but *you* die with me."

Ash processed the situation, still keeping the gun trained on Shafer. "Not if I shoot you and the bullet gets lodged inside your body. One rib is all it would take to slow it down, boy."

"Is that a risk you're willing to take?" Shafer moved even closer to the tank and spread out his arms. "Here's your chance. If you want to shoot me, do it now. I'm all yours."

Ash held the pistol with one hand. He wrapped his other hand around the first for extra stability, squinting one eye shut and aiming with the other. The barrel was locked on Shafer's chest.

Shafer's racing heartbeat pounded in his ears over the distant hum of the engine in the adjacent room. For what seemed like an eternity, he stopped breathing. *Had he pushed the limits?* If this is how it ended for him, he'd never know if the Brimley's got off the ship. He'd never see his aunt and uncle again.

He closed his eyes and waited for the gunshot and the pain. One question ricocheted through his mind over and over: *Was Ash crazy enough he was willing to risk his own life to end Shafer's?*

The answer, thankfully, was no.

With a sigh and grimace, Ash lowered the pistol and put it in his holster. "You're crazy, kid," he said.

Shafer exhaled in relief, offering, "I just had to even the odds, y'know?"

Ash widened his feet, balling his hands into fists and lifting them in front of his chest—a martial arts stance. "That's cute," he growled. "You actually think you have a chance?"

"I'm more likely to beat you than a *bullet*."

"Last time you tried to fight me, I knocked you out cold," Ash reminded him.

"And then you tried to kill me, and look where we're at now."

"Just stop yapping and fight."

Shafer raised both of his hands, trying to look like he knew what he was doing. "If you insist."

Even as the words left his mouth, he knew that without the element of surprise on his side this time, he was just about as likely to win this fight as he was to survive a gunshot at point-blank range. But winning wasn't on his mind. Instead, he was determined to do something else: he wanted to escape.

Ash charged. Instead of a sprint, it was more of a bouncing shuffle, keeping his fists raised and his elbows tucked in tight. He threw the first punch with his left hand, surprising Shafer, and the man's bare fist struck Shafer in the shoulder.

Shafer swore and recoiled, his arm throbbing and his still-weak collarbone bursting in pain. *Had he rebroken it?*

Ash was focused. He swung his right fist for Shafer's head, but Shafer ducked at the very last moment and felt what would have been a knock-out punch sail just over his head.

Ash was caught off-guard by the quick reaction. Shafer took advantage of the opening, throwing a punch of his own at his attacker's nose.

It came nowhere close to actually landing. For such an enormous man, Ash was incredibly quick. He grabbed Shafer's fist with both hands, whirled him around, then slammed him down on his back with an emphatic *crack!*

When Shafer crashed down into the cement, right beside the fallen body of Graf, he let out a groan. His eyes watered and pain radiated up his spine—so much so that he felt like it would never end. This might be his final resting place, right beside the soon-to-detonate bomb.

Then Ash reached for his pistol.

Shafer didn't have a choice. He *had* to move. Blinking back tears, he rolled to his chest and scrambled to his feet, hoping his back wouldn't give out on him in the process.

Pop! Pop! Ash fired two errant shots, both of which slammed into the wall.

In a mad dash, Shafer fought for traction on the cement floor as he ducked behind the fuel tank.

"Oh c'mon, not this again," Ash grumbled as he waited for Shafer to reappear.

"You're cheating!" Shafer hollered back, trying to

sound a lot stronger than he felt. "I thought we'd settled on a boxing match."

"In my line of work, there are no rules."

"Wait, you're a politician?"

"Funny." Ash began toward the fuel tank. As the sound of footsteps approached, Shafer made his next move. Staying as low as he could and out of sight, he darted forward. Just as Ash rounded the corner of the tank, Shafer slid out from behind it and made a break for the door.

"Hey!" Ash got off another shot, but he wasn't fast enough. The bullet dented the metal door as Shafer pulled it shut behind him.

"Way too close," Shafer muttered. Surely Ash was sprinting after him, so moving as quickly as he could, he snatched the *no-smoking* sign off the door and ran into the engine room.

With such a tremendous engine, the room was not only loud and hot, but it was also a maze. The engine had several different parts that snaked around the room and provided plenty of cover.

Shafer darted toward the far corner of the room, trying to hide behind part of the engine that would be out of sight for Ash. As he was about to claim the hiding spot, he saw a caution sign: *Hot steam released.*

No sooner had he seen the sign when a blast of steam shot out of the engine right over his would-have-been hiding place. If he hadn't seen the sign, he would have just been burned alive for sure.

But he wasn't in the clear yet.

The misstep sent him scrambling for another hiding spot. Still carrying the *no-smoking* sign, he ducked behind the central section of the engine. It wasn't the best hiding spot, but it was his only option. No sooner was he out of sight when the door flung open.

"Shafer, we can't do this forever," Ash yelled over the roar of the engine. "We're on the clock... literally."

Shafer held his breath, peering around the side of the engine and trying to spot Ash. When he did, he saw the hitman looking around with his pistol raised.

"What's the deal?" Ash taunted. "Are you all out of witty comments for me? Are you wanting to play hide-n-go seek? It's not a game you're going to win." He took a couple of steps to his right, closing in on Shafer.

Shafer wrapped his fingers around the sign in his hand, holding it like he would a frisbee. He had an idea, but it was by no means a good one. It was just his *only* one.

Ash took a couple more steps his way. In a matter of seconds, he would spot Shafer, and once that happened it would be all over.

Shafer made his move. Still crouched, he flung the sign across the room. It spun through the air just inches above the floor, clattering into the far wall.

At the sound, Ash spun too, whipping his pistol around and ready to pull the trigger. When he realized Shafer was nowhere to be seen, however, he muttered, "What the hell...?"

By the time he figured it out, it was too late. Shafer was already sprinting toward him. This time, Shafer's punch landed. This time, he drilled Ash in the back of the skull.

Ash jolted forward and he dropped the pistol, which skidded to the corner of the room. For just a moment while the man was dazed, Shafer knew he had a chance. He ran past Ash, making a move for the gun.

Ash recovered just in time to lunge forward as well.

Shafer dove. Throwing himself on the floor, he slid toward the pistol. If he could just get his hands on it, then he could win this battle.

His hand was six inches from the weapon when he came to an abrupt stop. Suddenly, there was pressure around his ankle. Ash had reached out with one enormous hand and clamped it around Shafer's leg.

"You've got to be kidding me," Shafer growled through gritted teeth. He abruptly kicked his leg, trying to break free.

Ash's grip didn't budge. If anything, it strengthened. He wrapped his other hand around Shafer's calf.

Shafer desperately reached out for the pistol one more time, but the swipe fell short.

"Good try, Shafer," Ash taunted as he began to drag Shafer away from the pistol.

Shafer clawed at the cement, but it was no use.

"I'm done with this," Ash went on. "No more games. I've let you put up a fight for long enough, but it's time to put an end to this. That's why I have to clip your wings."

"What are you..." Before Shafer could even get the question out, he figured out exactly what Ash meant. He felt the grip around his ankle begin to *twist*.

"Dammit—stop!" Shafer pleaded, jerking his body around violently as he tried to shake loose. As Ash twisted, more and more pressure built. It mounted so severely that an explosion seemed inevitable. Pain flashed in his eyes. All the air was sucked out of his lungs. All he could do was writhe and fight, until...

Pop!

It was over in a second, and Shafer screamed louder than he ever had in his life. The pain radiated up his leg, from his ankle to flashing blinding-white in his eyes.

Ash let go, and Shafer coiled his leg up, grabbing onto his ankle while continuing to scream. Tears ran down his cheeks and he shouted profanities as his vision flickered from the pain.

Ash was unphased. Cooly, he walked over to the pistol. "Shafer, you had a good run," he declared as he went. "You did. Taking down Blasnoff was impressive, but you pushed your luck a little too far this time."

Shafer silenced himself for just long enough to look at the man. To take in Ash and all of his smugness and confidence.

Ash bent over, picking up the pistol and admiring it like it was a championship trophy. He chuckled with pride. Then slowly, Ash raised the pistol and aimed it at Shafer, who was still clutching his ankle.

Once again, Shafer was staring down the barrel of a gun. But this time, if Ash pulled the trigger, there was no way he'd miss.

Shafer yelled, "Stop!" He held out both of his hands.

"What?" Ash refused to lower the gun. "You have some final words?"

"Yeah," Shafer nodded, tears running down his cheeks.

With one more smirk, Ash prompted. "Go on, then. Let's hear them, Shafer."

Very slowly, Shafer nodded. "You... you should've read the sign."

"What?" The word was barely a mumble, and by the

time Ash looked up to the *hot steam* sign posted behind him, it was too late. The valve opened up and a wave of the scalding steam blasted right into the man's face.

While Ash's vest might have been bulletproof, he was nowhere near prepared for what hit him. He screamed, but not like a human should scream. It was the sound of an animal. Ash threw his hands in front of his head, but by that point, it was too late. His skin was turning red and blistering so severely that he looked more like a monster from a horror movie than a man.

Still shrieking, he collapsed to the ground, and after a moment of writhing, the screams ended.

"I tried to tell you," Shafer panted as he grabbed a handrail and climbed to his feet. His ankle was swelling so much it fought with his shoe to escape. He tried to walk, only to decide it could only handle twenty percent of his weight, tops.

"Just what I need," he said through gritted teeth, limping over to the pistol but keeping his eyes away from the mess of Ash's body. "A bad ankle, a bomb to diffuse, and a solid seven flights of stairs to top it off."

As he scooped up the firearm, he hobbled into the fuel room and shut the door behind him so he could hear and think. He had no idea what he was going to do, but he knew he had to do *something*.

When he reached the bomb, he saw the timer: *24:11*. He was running out of time.

Once again, he studied the bomb. There was a vial of liquid. There were two wires. There was a timer and the rest of the frame. It meant nothing to him. In the movies, the hero usually cut one of the wires, but that was a huge risk, right? Perhaps a Hollywood gimmick, even.

Nevertheless, Shafer leaned in close and traced the wires with his eyes. One led from the vial to the side of the frame. The other connected the vial to the back of the frame.

Shafer wiped his sweaty brow. His head hurt. He leaned against the fuel tank, studying intently. *What do I do? Think, Shafer. Think.*

A familiar feeling stirred inside him. It wasn't a feeling of dread or worry, however, but more of a feeling of confusion. Once again, he felt like something was wrong. Something was off. The first time he'd studied the bomb, he'd felt the same way, but now the feeling was back and even stronger than before.

"What's going on? I know that…" He trailed off as slowly, piece-by-piece, the answer began to assemble in his head.

First, he thought about a couple of things that Graf had said. He thought about the situation—the layout of the room.

And suddenly he understood.

This bomb… wasn't a bomb.

For one thing, the explosive was so visible.. It could have been concealed a lot better, but instead, it was taped to the outside edge of the tank. Nothing discreet about it. If anything, it was almost as obvious as possible, like it was *meant* to be seen.

And Ash had killed a crewmember who had stumbled onto the scene doing *hourly maintenance*. The math didn't check out. Shafer was not sure how long the original timer on the bomb had been set for, but it had to have been well over a couple of hours, so surely Klaw would have anticipated some sort of hourly maintenance—

somebody would find the bomb long before it would ever explode.

But it was the last piece of the puzzle that truly tied everything together for Shafer, another bit that Graf had said: when the captain had signaled for help, his response was from three ships and a helicopter—a helicopter that probably shouldn't have been there, according to Graf.

As Shafer looked at the homemade explosive, he saw it with a new light, a new understanding: this "bomb" wasn't a bomb at all. It was a decoy. It was intended to be seen, which would trigger the outreach for help, which would be an open invitation for anybody in the area to come to the ship.

His stomach tightened. Suddenly, he felt sick.

There was a helicopter inbound, and Shafer would bet his life that one particular man was riding on it: Klaw.

That's the only thing that made sense. The killer. The mastermind behind all of this, who had manipulated Shafer, Graf, and even Ash, had devised a plan to be invited aboard the cruise ship to finish the job.

Shafer reached over to the bomb and jerked both of the wires loose. Nothing happened. The timer's clock continued to tick down, and his suspicions were confirmed. This was just a prop.

Even more nervous than before, Shafer began limping away from the fuel tank, heading to the stairs.

Klaw was coming, and if things went according to his plan, soon Stuart Brimley would be dead.

EIGHTEEN:
GOLDEN OCELOT MODE

Back in the engine room, Shafer quickly averted his gaze as he caught a glimpse of Ash's mangled body. With Ash out of the picture, his biggest priority was finding Mr. Brimley, letting him know what was going on, and getting him to safety.

It turned out, finding Mr. Brimley was much easier than anticipated.

As soon as he limped out of the engine room, he heard "Shafer?"

Shafer looked back in disbelief at Stuart Brimley, who was rushing down the stairs with concern plastered on his face.

"Stuart, what are you doing here?" Shafer asked. "How did you—"

"I saw you on the stairwell," Mr. Brimley answered. "And you were heading *down,* which didn't make much sense at first, but then I realized exactly where you were headed."

Shafer shrugged. "You're a clever man. I'm glad you're okay. Where's Heather and May?"

"I lost Heather in the process of getting everybody rounded up before the alarm sounded," he admitted. "But she's on the top deck, and she promised she'd load in a lifeboat."

"What about May?"

"She's good. I took her to the top deck and saw to it that she was safe."

"Then you came looking for me?"

"Exactly. I know what you said, but I couldn't abandon you here, Shafer."

Shafer shook his head. "You're a good guy, Stuart, but we've got to keep you safe. You can't die on my watch."

"I don't plan on it. Did you find the explosive?"

Shafer sighed. "Um... kinda. But there's a problem."

"What kind of problem?" Mr. Brimley asked. "Well, other than a bomb on the fuel tank..."

"That's just it... it's actually not a bomb at all." Shafer put his good ankle on the first stair and then brought the injured one up beside him. "The bomb was just a distraction. The whole point of it wasn't to detonate, but simply to be *seen*."

A puzzled look stretched across Mr. Brimley's face. "Why would they do that, Shafer? If they're trying to kill me, why *fake* an explosion?"

"Because it was meant to trigger a call for help. It worked, too--an SOS went out, and one of the first responders was a helicopter. I'd guess that helicopter is being flown by Klaw."

"Klaw is... the hitman?"

"Yeah. Ash, the other hitman, said that blowing up a ship seemed uncharacteristic for Klaw, and he was right. Blowing it up was never the point! I think he's using the chaos to get aboard the ship and kill you, and I'm thinking he'll try to make it look like an accident... or maybe just dump the body altogether."

Mr. Brimley processed everything, looking down at the floor. "That's... that's a lot. Doesn't that seem like a stretch?"

"I mean, kinda," Shafer admitted. "But I'd say I'm ninety-five percent certain. If the bomb was real, I just diffused it, but I don't think it should have been that easy."

Suddenly Mr. Brimley looked over Shafer's head, peering to the back of the engine room to the lump of scorched, oozing flesh. His eyes widened. "Is that... Szalay? Or Ash? Or... whoever."

Shafer nodded.

"Did you... *kill* him?"

"I, um... he kinda killed himself."

Mr. Brimley shook his head. "Shafer, I had no idea. I'm so sorry... I should have been here."

"No, that's the point," Shafer insisted. "If all of this was put into place to kill you, then you need to be as far from harm's way as possible. You shouldn't have come looking for me, even—that just plays into Klaw's plan."

Mr. Brimley nodded reluctantly. "Yeah... you're right."

"I know. And that's why you've got to stay here. I'm sure Heather and May are safe. They're both probably on the lifeboats by now. So you have to stay *right here*. You're a businessman genius, so I know you realize this gives us the best odds of keeping you safe, right?"

"Yeah."

Shafer turned around, hobbling over to Ash's body. "And that gives me an idea. Come here."

Mr. Brimley hurried over to Shafer. "What's going on? What can I do?"

"Help me get this off... never mind, I got it." Trying not to touch Ash's burned flesh, Shafer unfastened the seared kevlar vest and slipped it off. "Take this."

Mr. Brimley took the vest from Shafer and shook his head. "Shafer, no. I don't need—"

"If a *hitman* wants you dead, you need all the layers of protection you can get." Shafer reached over and plucked a piece of burned flesh from the material, wiping it on the floor. "See, good as new."

Mr. Brimley grimaced, then hung the vest on the rail beside him. "I think I'll take my chances."

"C'mon. It's not that bad..."

"Shafer, I'm staying here. Remember? I'll be fine."

"Okay, okay," Shafer caved. "But you gotta do that. I'm going to go take care of things, then I'll come back for you, Stuart. Just stay here. *Promise me.*"

After hesitation, a scowling Mr. Brimley nodded. "Yes. This is just hard, Shafer. I shouldn't be sending a *boy* out to fight my battles. What are you going to do?"

Shafer held up the pistol he'd taken from Ash. "Maybe use this. I have no idea, honestly. But I'll figure it out. I always do."

"I don't like this," Mr. Brimley said. "Not at all."

"I know. But you're doing the right thing."

A long pause came. "Fine, Shafer. But my parental

instincts are telling me this is the worst idea I've ever had."

"Then it's a good thing the computer science genius part of your brain is telling you to listen to logic instead," Shafer replied. "I'll be back when it's safe. I'm going Golden Ocelot mode."

"Good luck," Mr. Brimley responded, but his voice sounded like his body was fighting his brain. "I'll... I'll be here."

"Good." Shafer turned to leave but was stopped.

"Hey, Shafer?"

"Yeah?"

"Do you know what this Klaw person looks like? I need to be on the lookout."

"Oh, yeah." Shafer remembered something else he hadn't told Mr. Brimley. "We've actually both seen him before."

"Wait, *really*? How?"

"He was pretending to be your new groundsman. Remember Sylvio?"

Suddenly Mr. Brimley turned white and his jaw dropped open. "No. No! That's... no."

Shafer nodded, surprised by the reaction. "I thought the same thing at first, but it only makes sense."

Mr. Brimley shook his head. "Not what I mean. Shafer, we've got to go—*now!* This is bad. This is really bad."

"Bad? What's bad?" Seeing Mr. Brimley finally lose his composure made Shafer's stomach lurch.

"On the main evacuation deck, when I was up there with May..." Mr. Brimley was suddenly talking a hundred words a minute. "A man was calling to us, saying he could help. I thought he was part of the crew because I knew I'd seen him before, and I sent her to him before I came back down here, but..."

As Shafer realized what Mr. Brimley was saying, his heart began to race. "Stuart... are you saying that Klaw has May?"

After a long, empty silence, Mr. Brimley nodded. "He took her by the hand, and... Dammit, Shafer, I handed my daughter over to a killer."

The words left Shafer feeling like he'd been torn in two.

"We've gotta get up there," Mr. Brimley said. "If he has May..." He never finished the thought. He didn't need to.

Shafer, in contemplative silence, began to slowly make his way up the stairs. Through a wince, he managed, "If Klaw has May, it's to get to you," he said. "You still have to stay here, Stuart. He won't hurt May. He only wants you."

"Shafer, you don't sound very certain."

Shafer stopped, looking down at his throbbing ankle. "I'm... well... I'm going to save her."

Suddenly surprised, Mr. Brimley asked, "Good heavens, what happened to your ankle? I... I just noticed."

"Ash... he twisted it."

"Is it broken?"

"No, just sprained. I think."

"Shafer, it's huge. No way you can make it up the stairs."

Shafer insisted. "No, I've got to. There's not a choice."

Mr. Brimley thought about this for just a moment, then said, "If we could get you up two stories, I know there's an elevator."

"You're supposed to—"

"Shafer, I'm not staying down here if he has my *daughter*. Now it's personal. He can kill me, for all I care. But I need May to be safe."

Shafer let out a long, reluctant sigh, then changed the topic. "Aren't the elevators shut down for evacuation?"

"Maybe they should be, but I saw people were using them to get to the evacuation deck."

"Then why the hell did we take the stairs all the way down here..." Shafer grumbled, then locked eyes with Mr. Brimley. "Fine. Let's do it. Help me get to that elevator, but that's as far as you go. I'll do the rest." He tried to take another step up the next stair, but winced and cried out.

Mr. Brimley came to the rescue, bending down beside Shafer. "Put your arm around me. Use me like a crutch."

"Thanks," Shafer growled in pain as he did as told. With Mr. Brimley supporting quite a bit of his weight on one side and a handrail on the other, they began climbing up the stairs.

It hurt. It hurt more than Shafer could have ever anticipated, and if he wasn't motivated by the thought of saving May, he couldn't have done it. There was no way he would have scraped up the willpower to climb the stairs.

But he did, and she was the only thing he could think about the entire way. Ash was dead and the bomb was defused, but things were far from over. Something bad was coming—he could feel it.

After lots of pain and groans, Shafer made it to the top of the stairs and headed down the long hallway, passing by empty staff cabins. "Where is that elevator?" He broke free of Mr. Brimley, forcing himself to walk on his own.

Mr. Brimley, hovering nearby if needed, said, "Just down here and on the left."

By the time they reached the elevator, Shafer was praying that it was still online. If not, he was out of luck. He couldn't go on, not like this.

He punched the button to summon it, and to his relief, it glowed to life.

As they waited, a beep came from overhead and an announcement came from speakers in the ceiling. It wasn't the repeating announcement of evacuation policies, however. It was different.

Over the intercom, a calm male voice announced, "Stuart Brimley, please report to the lido deck. We have your daughter."

Shafer and Mr. Brimley looked at each other immediately, both turning pale. The announcement was a deceptive one: it sounded friendly. Innocent. Most people who heard it would have thought that a member of the crew was trying to reunite separated family members.

Shafer, however, knew otherwise, and hearing the announcement confirmed his worst suspicions: Klaw was already one step ahead of them.

This announcement was a threat.

"Once again, Stuart Brimley, please come to the lido deck," the voice repeated. "We have your daughter."

"Shafer…" Mr. Brimley couldn't seem to find the words. "This is all my fault. What is Heather going to say?"

"She's not going to say anything, because I'm going to get May back," Shafer answered. He readjusted his grip on the pistol. "Try not to worry. You won't think straight if you're worried."

"You're right." Mr. Brimley nervously ran his free hand through his hair. "It's just hard, Shafer."

"Yeah, I know." There was a beep from the elevator, and the doors slid open. Shafer hobbled inside.

Behind him, Mr. Brimley asked, "So what's the plan? What do we do once we get to the lido deck?"

As Shafer turned around to face Mr. Brimley, he knew what he had to do, and the thought made his knees weak. Slowly, he shook his head. "Stuart, you heard what I said. *We* are not going to the lido deck… I am."

Mr. Brimley immediately objected. "No, Shafer. No! I can't let you do that. You heard that announcement—he has *my* daughter."

Shafer spread his hands across the entrance of the elevator, blocking the entry. "I'm sorry, Stuart, but nothing has changed. You've gotta stay here. Klaw's not after me. He's after you."

"Shafer, move. Don't be ridiculous." A flash of anger boiled in Mr. Brimley's voice.

Since Shafer had met Mr. Brimley, there had been nothing but friendship between them. Respect. A bond, even. And that's why directly defying Mr. Brimley was nearly too much for Shafer, but he stuck to his guns.

"Stuart, *stay here*." Shafer's voice was just as edgy and insistent. "You gotta stay here."

Mr. Brimley stepped forward. "Shafer, I'm serious. Let me on that elevator this very instant."

Shafer argued, "I don't know why, but Klaw wants me alive. He's here to kill *you*. Do you not get that?"

"May's *my* daughter," Mr. Brimley half-pleaded, half-shouted. "Do *you* not understand?"

"I do. And that's exactly why I'm going to go save her and bring her back to you."

"Let me… *on*!" Mr. Brimley stepped forward and shoved Shafer as the doors began to close.

"No!" Shafer shoved Mr. Brimley back, sending him staggering into the hallway. "Stuart, I'm so sorry, but trust me. You've gotta trust me."

"No!" Mr. Brimley tried again, but it was too late. The doors were nearly shut. "No! Shafer! No!"

As the door closed, the desperation in Mr. Brimley's voice left Shafer shaking from what he'd just done. He was easily on track to be the worst possible future son-in-law of all time.

Letting out a long, choppy breath, Shafer pressed the *10* button. With a lurch, the elevator began to rise.

It was the longest ride of his life. As he ascended all the way to the lido deck, all Shafer could do was think: he thought about what was waiting for him at the top, about who he'd betrayed and left at the bottom, and how bad his ankle was throbbing.

More than anything, though, he tried to think up a plan.

For just a moment, Shafer closed his eyes and thought back to his brief time working in the field with the FBI. If nothing else, he'd taken two things away from that mission: always come in with a thorough plan, and always be ready to improvise if things went to hell.

At least he was good at the second.

His biggest concern, though—the one that made his heart race like it was poised to explode out of his chest—was May. Klaw had taken her for a reason, and as long as he had May, he had all the leverage in the world, leverage he could use over both Mr. Brimley *and* Shafer.

Shafer rubbed his thumb along the grip of the pistol. "You can do this," he told himself. You've got to do this. You're… the Golden Ocelot."

The words brought calmness and memories of May. He'd faced long-shot odds before and come out on top, so he could do that again. For her.

The elevator's light flashed deck seven. This was it. He was getting close. He had to come up with *something* he could do.

There was no such luck. He watched the elevator dial turn to eight, nine, then stop altogether.

There was a ding, and the doors began to slide open.

This was it. He took a deep breath: it was time to face Klaw.

NINETEEN:
SHOTS FIRED

As the elevator doors slid open and Shafer sighed. He knew he shouldn't approach Klaw with a pistol in hand, so he tucked the gun in the back of his pants then made a swipe down all of the buttons on the elevator, pressing every floor. Mr. Brimley would be trying to follow, so Shafer needed all the time he could get.

After a deep breath, he walked from the elevator to the lido deck and began to survey the surroundings. It took no time to spot the helicopter. It was on the very top deck of the ship. Sleek and black, it was probably a six-seater. Below, on the lido deck, Shafer looked for Klaw.

He wasn't hard to find, either. Klaw looked almost exactly like Shafer remembered. He was beside the pool, sitting atop one of the tables with his feet on the bench seat. Wearing all black, he had a pistol laid across his lap.

May was there too, but very obviously not by choice. A gag was tied around her mouth and her wrists were bound. She was sitting in a lawn chair, rigid with fear. Even at a distance, Shafer could see her shoulders quickly rising and falling as she took shaky breaths.

Klaw was the first to spot Shafer, but May followed closely behind. She instinctively popped to her feet, but Klaw scooped the pistol from his lap and aimed it at her. "Not so fast, princess. Take a seat."

Slowly, reluctantly, she dropped back down in the lawn chair.

"Hey," Shafer greeted. "How about you stop pointing the gun at her?"

Klaw turned the pistol away from May, aiming it instead at Shafer. "Shafer McCartney! What an unexpected surprise!"

"Good to see you too, Sylvio," Shafer shot back. "What are you doing here? Did you finish pruning all the rose bushes at the Brimley's?"

Klaw laughed, and as far as Shafer could tell, it was an authentic laugh. Nothing forced. Nothing sinister. "You're good, Shafer," he answered.

"And you're not Italian," Shafer pointed out, noticing the accent he associated with Klaw had vanished.

"No, I'm one of *yours*," Klaw proclaimed. "But I must say that I'm honored you decided to drop by and say hello when there's a bomb to diffuse."

Shafer continued limping across the lido deck. "I figured out your plan as soon as I saw the bomb," he said. "Somebody with your reputation wouldn't plan anything so likely to fail unless it was *intended* to fail."

Klaw gave May a quick glance, then replied, "I'm flattered you think so much of my work, Shafer."

"I'm just going off what your good pal Ash told me."

Klaw nodded. "He's always one to 'hype me up,' as you kids say it."

"For one, you're not using that right, and two, he's dead, so you're gonna need a new hypeman soon," Shafer relayed.

This seemed to catch Klaw by surprise, but he made a great effort not to show it. "He's... dead. Now how did that happen?"

"He tried to kill me while I was attempting to diffuse the bomb."

Klaw seemed to process the words. He chuckled then asked, "Is that how you hurt your ankle? My boy, you're moving terribly."

"Nah, I'm fine. No worries at all, thanks."

Klaw repositioned his grip on the pistol, aiming it even more intently on Shafer, and said, "Well if that's the case, then I'm going to go out on a limb and say your awkward upright walking position is because you have a pistol shoved in the back of your pants."

"I lied," Shafer corrected quickly. "It's the ankle. It hurts really bad. Like a nine-out-of-ten bad. It's maybe even broken."

"Shafer, please set down your firearm." Klaw's voice was insistent. "I've been doing this for far too long for you to come up here and John McClane me."

"Who?"

"Just surrender your weapon."

Shafer stopped, leaning against a nearby chair to take some of the weight off his ankle. After a moment of hesitation, he reluctantly pulled the pistol from his pants and lowered it to the deck.

"Thanks, Shafer. Now kick it to me."

"You're very annoying." Shafer reluctantly kicked his only lifeline away. It skidded across the deck before coming to rest at Klaw's feet.

Lowering his own gun now, Klaw said, "I've never competed for the title of everybody's favorite contract killer. I just do a good job and get paid. I'm not here to make friends."

"That sure is a good thing."

Klaw stood up, stepping down from the bench seat. "Speaking of the job, where's Stuart? I'm sure you both heard my announcement, so I can't help but wonder why I'm talking to a child instead of a software guru right now."

"Stuart's busy at the moment," Shafer answered.

Klaw turned to May. "Ah, do you hear that? Daddy's too busy to come to save you."

"He's too busy staying alive," Shafer added. "And that's why I'm here."

"To save... what's your name, honey? May?"

Through the gag, she replied with two muffled words, but Shafer suspected she wasn't answering the question.

Klaw lowered his own pistol and beckoned Shafer forward. "Come, sit. You need to get some weight off that ankle. I can see the swelling from here."

"I'll be fine," Shafer insisted as he slowly approached Klaw. He and May met eyes for just a moment. "Can you clear up something for me, Klaw?"

Klaw smirked. "What do you want to know?"

Shafer looked down to his leg, examining the bruise

that was spreading along the outside of his ankle. "Why did you decide to use the fake bomb? Wouldn't it have been easier to just *go through* with the plan and blow up the ship rather than go through all this work?"

Klaw bit his lip. He looked out to the ocean for just a moment, where a couple of lifeboats were rising and falling. Then, returning his attention to the conversation, he asked, "Shafer, do you think I'm a monster?"

"A... wait, is that a trick question?"

"No. Answer it."

"I... um... yes."

"Why?"

Shafer thought. "I... I don't know much about you." He took a couple of steps forward. "But what I know now is this: you've killed a lot of people and you've spent the last few weeks trying to kill my girlfriend's father. That's not a great first impression."

"You say '*trying*' like you don't think I'm going to do it."

Shafer ignored him. "So yeah, I think you're a monster." He limped two more steps closer, cutting his eyes once more to a terrified May.

Sarcastically, Klaw held a hand to his heart. "Shafer, I'm hurt. Truly." He pointed out toward the lifeboats bobbing in the ocean and asked, "Do you not realize why I used a fake bomb? Think about it."

Shafer didn't answer.

"Because I didn't want to kill *everybody*," Klaw insisted. "I'm not trying to cause harm, just... well... do a job. That's how it is. That's how it's always been. I'm not the bad guy in this story. I'm not the villain that wants Stuart Brimley dead—I'm just the person with the brains and talent to make it happen."

"You're wrong…"

Klaw went on. "So, to answer your question, the point of the fake explosive was to *save* everybody else so I could get on board, kill Stuart, and sink his body to the very bottom of the ocean. The media would have loved the story about the heroic billionaire who drowned trying to save a young child who fell overboard during the evacuation, and I have it ready to leak."

Shafer struggled to believe what he was hearing. "Are you hearing yourself right now? That's a twisted view! I don't care how much money we're talking about… you're willing to end a human life for it."

In a flash, Klaw whipped his head to Shafer. As they locked gazes, Klaw said, "Seventy-five million dollars, Shafer."

"What?"

"That was the price tag for this hit, with the stipulation that I could make it look like an accident. Enough money that I'd never have to work again. I'd never have to *kill* again. Stuart Brimley will be my last victim, then I can retire and golf, fish, or even hunt—animals, of course."

"I was gonna ask."

Klaw looked back down at the pistol in his hand. "Let me ask you this, Shafer. How far would you go for seventy-five million dollars? For never having to work a day in your life?"

After a long pause, Shafer responded, "I wouldn't kill for it."

Klaw looked back into his eyes. "You couldn't possibly sound more uncertain, Shafer." He laughed like it had been a funny joke. "Here's the thing: You and I, we're not that different. We both have talent, wit, and we're good at figuring out the world around us. The difference between us is that you think you're using your abilities for good, and I'm using mine to make a living."

Now it was Shafer's turn to laugh, which came out as more of a huff of disbelief. "If that's what you have to tell yourself to sleep at night, then do it."

Klaw raised his gun again and his expression became a little sharper, more threatening. "Shafer, I'm losing my patience. Tell me where Stuart Brimley is, or I'll put a bullet in your girlfriend and make you watch her die."

As the gun swung toward May, she froze. Silent tears ran down her cheeks. She sniffled while staring with wide eyes.

Shafer held out a hand. "No, don't shoot her. If you're gonna shoot anybody, shoot me."

The gun turned back to Shafer. "Give me Stuart, Shafer. That's all I ask. Nobody else has to die today."

Shafer kept his hands out to show he meant no harm, and channeling his inner liar, he said, "I… I don't know where Stuart is." He threw a little quiver in his voice, just for authenticity.

"I don't believe—"

"I was down with the bomb," Shafer insisted, "And as soon as I'd diffused it, I heard the announcement you made. I came straight here, all by myself."

Klaw shook his head. "Shafer, please. You can barely stand on your own—I know you didn't make it up to the elevator as a one-man band."

Dammit. The curse rang inside Shafer's head. Klaw was onto him, and he was quickly running out of options. Talking was getting him nowhere, and he didn't have any more backup plans. At this point, there was only one thing he had left to try.

He had to attack.

His only hope was that Klaw, for whatever reason, wouldn't kill him. That's what Ash had said, and if that was true, it could level the odds.

Shafer took a deep breath, looking one last time into Klaw's face and locking on to his intelligent eyes. "You want the truth?"

"Nothing but it."

"The truth is…" He tensed, preparing to spring to action. "The truth is… you're never getting Stuart!" With that, lunged straight as Klaw—straight at the pistol, even.

It turned out, Ash had been right. If Klaw had been willing to kill Shafer, he had every chance to do it, but instead of firing the pistol, he lowered it.

Shafer led his attack with a wild punch, which Klaw deflected with his off-hand.

Spinning on his good leg, Shafer squared up to Klaw, hands raised. He'd seen the man before, but this was the first time he'd truly sized him up. While Ash had been bulky and strong, Klaw was built much differently. He was slim, wiry, and toned.

Klaw holstered the pistol on his belt, lifting his other hand and crossing it in front of his body, palm open. He bent at the knees, prepared to either attack or evade.

Meanwhile, Shafer could barely stand. His ankle was throbbing insistently. But he had to. This was his only option.

Shuffling forward with his good leg driving his weight, he tried to uppercut Klaw, but as quick as a cat, Klaw blocked the punch, spun Shafer around with a kick, and then effortlessly slung him down to the deck.

As Shafer landed on his already-sore tailbone, he shouted in pain, and when it finally resided, he asked, "What the hell was that?"

"Did I not mention I'm a blackbelt?" Klaw asked, thoughtfully. "Also a red belt to the ninth degree, but I'm not sure if you follow jiu-jitsu."

Shafer couldn't respond. He just laid on the deck, staring up at the sky and trying to find the willpower to get back to his feet. At this point, he wasn't sure if he even could. His entire leg burned like it was on fire, his spine tingled, and together it was so much that he felt his brain trying to shut off. Trying to escape.

Klaw reached out a hand. "Want some help getting to your feet? I'm not sure if we're done fighting or not. Have you had your fill of playing hero for the day, or do you want another round?"

Shafer groaned.

To his right, he saw May stand up once again, but without even looking away from Shafer, Klaw drew the pistol and aimed it at her. "No helping your boyfriend. That's cheating," he scolded.

As Shafer fought to keep his watery eyes open, he considered everything he'd been through—all the times he should have died— and couldn't shake a particular thought from his head. A question. A suspicion.

"Hey, Klaw?" Forming the words was a struggle in its own right.

"Yes?"

"Why me?" He opened his eyes again.

Klaw stood over him, staring down in confusion. "What are you talking about?"

Shafer tried to roll over, but he groaned as a sharp pain stabbed his back. "Why won't you kill me?"

Klaw chuckled. "Why do you say that? Maybe I'm just relishing the moment."

Shafer slowly and painfully shook his head. "No. Ash said you ordered me to be spared. And I can tell by the way you're acting, too. You could have shot me, here and now."

"Would you like me to?" Klaw lifted the gun, but it came across as an empty threat.

"I just want to know why. Why me? You had no problem with killing May and Heather when you tried to gas Stuart in his sleep, but you wanted me kept safe. *Why me?*" He repeated.

There was a moment of complete silence, save the distant lapping of waves against the ship far below and the occasional shouts from the evacuation. Finally, Klaw answered, "I see a lot of myself in you, Shafer."

"I don't know about—"

"Our priorities are different, of course, but we're much alike. You could do so much more than you're letting yourself do."

"You... you're saying you want to turn me into a hitman?" Even saying the words felt ridiculous.

"I'm saying the option will always be open if you want to learn from the best."

"Do you know who my uncle is? Do you know who you're talking to?"

"Oh, I know Richard McCartney very well. We've had some run-ins before, I assure you."

"Rich knows *you?*" Shafer leaned forward, crying out from the effort, but managed to prop himself up with his elbow. "How do you know my uncle?"

Ding. An unexpected sound came from across the lido deck, and as soon as Shafer heard it, his heart sunk. He knew exactly what it was, and more than that, he knew what was going to happen.

Klaw heard it too, and smiling, he turned from Shafer to the source of the noise.

To the elevator.

The doors opened, and very slowly, Stuart Brimley walked out of them. He had his hands raised, walking with short, innocent steps. "Hey!" he called out. "It's me you want. Take me, and let my daughter and Shafer go."

"No!" Shafer yelled. "Stuart, get out of here! He's not going to—"

He was cut off by May, who suddenly began sprinting toward her father.

Mr. Brimley didn't stop. He slowly advanced toward May, coming out onto the deck like a sacrificial lamb. Klaw's pistol was trained on him.

But, in his focus on Mr. Brimley, Klaw made a mistake. He'd let his guard down. He'd turned his back on Shafer.

Seeing the opening, Shafer forced himself up, grabbing onto a table leg for support as he hoisted himself to his feet. But he moved slowly. So slowly. His body refused to cooperate as he tried to steady his feet and charge Klaw. But he couldn't run—at most, it was a painful limp.

Still, he powered forward. He reached out to the hitman. He tried to save Mr. Brimley.

He never made it.

Bang!

The single gunshot exploded on the lido deck. May

shrieked into the gag, continuing forward in a mad scramble, running to her father.

Mr. Brimley staggered backward. Reaching a hand to the gunshot wound on his chest, he looked at May then toward Klaw. The dazed look on his face suggested his brilliant brain couldn't process what had just happened.

May continued forward, madly, but she wasn't quick enough. Mr. Brimley dropped before she reached him, collapsing onto the deck.

"No!" Shafer screamed out. "No! Stuart!" He dove into Klaw, plowing his shoulder into the man's chest, but Klaw managed to shake loose and sent Shafer hopping one-legged across the deck.

Across the deck, May was holding her father's limp body. Mr. Brimley's eyes were still open and he stared emptily at the sky above them. May grabbed her father with her bounded wrists, laying him across her lap. Through the gag, she let out delusional, garbled screams. Was she begging him to breathe? To be alive?

Whatever she was saying, it was no use.

May's screams turned into wild sobs—tears of agony as she held onto her father.

Shafer couldn't believe what he was seeing, but he couldn't force himself to look away. When he did, he spotted Klaw striding toward the helicopter.

In a rage, Shafer shouted, "You're not walking away from this, Klaw! You… you killed Stuart!"

Klaw stopped, looking back over his shoulder. "Don't seem so surprised. I told you all along that I was going to—you knew it was coming."

In response, Shafer charged forward, adrenaline propelling him to the point that the pain in his ankle barely registered. At that point, he only wanted one thing: to kill Klaw.

But before he ever reached Klaw, Shafer was blown off his feet by a thunderous impact, slamming down to the deck. He landed on his ribs, knocking all the air out of his lungs, and looked up into the sun to face the new attacker.

As his eyes adjusted, Shafer couldn't believe what he was seeing.

With a swollen eye, torn clothing, and burned, blistered skin, Ash glared down at him with pure hatred in his eyes. His shoulders rose and fell violently like every breath was laborious, but somehow, he was alive.

"Ah, Ash!" Klaw exclaimed. "I always knew you were tough to kill. You really do look like hell, though."

Ash didn't respond. Instead, he jumped on top of Shafer, leaned in close enough that Shafer could smell all the burned flesh.

Ash shouted, "Do you see what you did to me, you little bastard?" Spit spewed as he yelled. "I'm going to kill you! I'm going to kill you and your girlfriend and your family…"

Once again, Ash clamped his hands around Shafer's throat. This time, however, was different. This time, he was squeezing with intent, like he was trying to separate Shafer's head from his shoulders.

He was squeezing to kill.

Shafer opened his mouth, but a gurgle was the only noise that escaped. He couldn't breathe. The grip around his neck was too much. The pressure was building. His head was spinning. The light was fading. Much like his ankle, he could tell his neck was ready to snap at any second.

The light—what was left of it—trickled away. The cold hand of death was closing in. Shafer could feel it. He could hear shouts, but not make out their words. All his senses were dying. *He* was dying.

Bang! Bang! Bang! Three shots sounded, and in the lifeless darkness, Shafer could feel warm, wet liquid splatter all over him. The pressure on his neck lessened, and as air returned to his lungs, bringing with it partial vision, he saw three separate pools of blood spreading across Ash's chest.

Ash's face, or what was left of the burned flesh, looked surprised. His mouth was wide open, but no sound came out. Only blood. Then, almost as suddenly as he had attacked, he collapsed to the deck, rolling off Shafer.

But for Shafer, it was too late. He couldn't catch his breath. He couldn't get in enough air, and between the lack of oxygen and the pain, his brain was shutting down.

Once again, he couldn't move. He couldn't see. He could only hear and feel.

Across the deck, the sound of May's wailing was unbroken, relentless, and gut-wrenching. Soon, that was all Shafer could hear. The broken cries consumed him.

But before he lost consciousness, a strange sensation overtook him. With the darkness closing in around him, he felt his hand lifted up. His arm was extended, and there was a light touch against his skin. Against his wrist.

Was it being sliced? No, this was something else. A brush. Something gentle. Something soft. Lines were being brushed on the inside of his wrist, but from who or for what, he had no idea.

As quickly as it started, the sensation stopped. Sha-

fer's hand dropped back to the deck, and footsteps resumed.
    Footsteps and screams.
    Then he was out.

TWENTY:
FROM THE GRAVE

"Shafer? Can you hear me?"

Shafer's eyes fluttered open. "Rich?"

"Shafer! Thank God you're ok."

Locking his blurry vision onto his uncle's face, Shafer asked, "How did you get here?"

Leaning back, Richard McCartney forced a smile. He looked tired, like he was running on fumes. "I have connections. When I heard that your ship was in trouble, I used them."

"Where am I?"

"A Dominican hospital."

"Where's June?"

"On an inbound plane."

Shafer was in bed, partially covered by a sheet, and he pulled his ankle out from underneath it to examine. Not only was it enormous, but the bruising climbed up his leg. He tried to extend his toes, but everything was far too swollen for them to move.

Rich noticed. "You've got a grade-three ankle sprain," he explained. "Some ligament tearing. You'll probably get fitted for a brace when the swelling goes down."

"Okay."

"How did it happen, Shafer?"

Shafer looked down at his ankle. He couldn't bring himself to even begin to address the question. Instead, he said the one word that was heavy on his mind: "Stuart." After a pause to collect, he added, "Stuart's... dead."

"I'm... *what?*" The question came from outside the room, and through the door walked a grinning Stuart Brimley. One of his shoulders was in a sling, and May was wrapped around his other arm. Her eyes were puffy but dry, and she was clutching Mr. Brimley so tightly she looked like she'd never let him go.

Shafer did a double-take. "What... you're... you're dead." He couldn't take his eyes off the ghost of the man standing at the foot of his bed. "I saw Klaw shoot you... He..."

Mr. Brimley shook his head. "Yeah, he did."

"I don't understand..."

Mr. Brimley grinned. "Well, you *should*. I'm alive because of your idea, Shafer."

All the gears were turning in Shafer's head, and suddenly he understood. "The bulletproof vest!"

"Exactly."

"But... but you weren't wearing it. I saw you with my own eyes. There was no vest."

"It was under my shirt, Shafer." Mr. Brimley opened his shirt at the collar, revealing a nasty bruise on his chest.

"See here? The magic of Kevlar."

"I can't believe…"

"When you pushed me out of the elevator, you know what I did?"

"You went and got that vest…?"

Mr. Brimley nodded. "Yes. But more than that, I got to thinking about what you said, and I realized something… as much as I hated it as a father, I knew you were right."

Shafer was too stunned to even speak.

Mr. Brimley went on. "But I also knew I couldn't leave you to face Klaw alone, so just like you suggested, I put on the vest and went upstairs." After a pause, he added, "But when I made it back to the engine room, I noticed that Captain Szalay was gone, so I figured he must not have been dead after all. That only made me double my efforts to get up to you, and, well… get shot."

Shafer took everything in for a moment, then asked. "But when you were shot, I saw you. You were… dead."

Mr. Brimley gave another grin and rubbed the back of his head. With a chuckle, he admitted, "Um… this is the embarrassing part. Getting shot was worse than I expected, and it knocked me down. On the way down, I hit my head on the deck—knocked me out cold."

"But… I thought…" Shafer closed his eyes and rubbed his face. "Never mind. I'm just glad you're standing in my room."

Mr. Brimley squeezed May's shoulders. "Shafer, you saved me. Your quick thinking overpowered my stubbornness, and that's the only reason why I'm here."

Shafer dropped his gaze to his bedsheet. "I'm sorry about what I did at the elevator."

Mr. Brimley shook his head. "You were in the right, and I was the one being stupid. Shafer, *thank you* for what you did there."

"That nearly tore me apart, just so you know," Shafer admitted. "So... you're still good with me dating your daughter?"

Mr. Brimley gave him a toothy smile. "Only if you promise to keep saving our lives."

"Maybe you need to stop getting on everybody's blacklist," Shafer countered, finally giving the slightest of smiles.

Mr. Brimley laughed. "Heather told me the same exact thing. And that reminds me, I gotta go check on her."

May stood up, squeezing Shafer's hand along the way. There were no words spoken between them, but there didn't need to be. Shafer could feel everything.

She and her father left, leaving Shafer in much better spirits. "Stuart's... alive." He said the words like he couldn't believe them, like he needed confirmation.

Rich nodded.

Shafer looked around. "I can't believe this. Any of it. I... I... I've got to stop waking up in random hospital beds."

Rich reached out and rubbed a hand through Shafer's hair, messing it up just the way Shafer hated. "Then I guess you've got to stop saving the world."

"This one... this wasn't me."

"It was though," Rich insisted. "To hear Stuart tell it, you were the only reason the whole Brimley family is alive in the first place. I just wish I knew everything that happened from the time you set foot on the boat."

Shafer shook his head, playfully swatting away his

uncle's hand and fixing his hair. "Listen, I still have *tons* of questions, and I should get to go first."

"Fire away."

Shafer tried to figure out where to begin. "Ash is really dead, right?"

"Frederick Urban, you mean."

"Who?"

"A notorious criminal who's had his hand in several illegal operations." Rich rubbed his chin. "He's also the man that you burned with hot steam?"

"Frederick Urban?" Shafer whispered the name to himself, trying it out. "Yeah, that's the guy, but I knew him as 'Ash.' Honestly, I can't blame him for going by that if his real name's *Frederick*. That's awful."

Rich took out a notebook and flipped it open. "Stuart said that you and Urban got into a fight in the engine room. I'll have to hear about that later."

"Deal. But is he dead?"

"He is now."

Shafer nodded, thankful. "So… did Klaw get away?"

"Klaw." There was recognition in Rich's voice. "He did. All trails are cold."

"Dammit."

"We'll keep looking." Rich glanced out the window as he let out a long exhalation. "We always do."

"So it's true," Shafer said. "You know Klaw. He said you had chased him before."

Richard turned back to Shafer. "You talked to him, Shafer?"

"Yes."

"What did he tell you?"

"Um…" Shafer thought back to the conversation.

"He said you've had some run-ins with each other. Why?"

Mr. Brimley rubbed his chin. "I... I've been trying to catch that man for years. He's the one who got away." Looking back to Shafer, he forced a smile. "I can tell you those stories another time. I've heard something else about you and Klaw that caught my attention. You said he wouldn't kill you...?"

Shafer nodded.

"How did you know that?"

"I overheard him talking to Ash, and Ash kept promising that I wouldn't be harmed. Klaw wanted me spared."

"But you don't know why?"

He paused for a long while, debating how to answer. Finally, he offered. "Not really."

"Did you ask?"

"Yeah, and well, I don't know." Shafer thought back to the brief conversation on the lido deck. "His answer was really weird, though. He said he believes I've got talent and he sees himself in me. I guess that's enough to want to spare me?"

"Apparently."

Shafer looked his uncle in the eyes. "The hit... who wanted to kill Stuart?"

To his surprise, Rich only shook his head and said, "The Bureau is on the hunt. We're turning over every stone, and we will find who did this."

"So you don't know?"

"Not yet."

Shafer exhaled, closing his eyes and leaning his head back into the pillow. He thought about everything, from the high-speed car ride to the final fistfight, and he knew he shouldn't have been here. He should have been dead a dozen times over.

But something else popped into his mind. Another memory. Something from those final moments, lying there and blacking out: he'd felt something on his wrist. He'd felt something brushing against him.

Immediately, Shafer pulled his right hand from under the covers, turned it over, and looked at the inside of his wrist. Across his skin, one word was written in black, permanent marker. It was smudged like water had gotten ahold of it, but after a moment, he made out one word: *Gobert.*

He read it, then he read it again. *What was this? What did it mean?* Even stranger than the word, though, was another question: *who wrote this on his arm?* As Shafer thought back to what happened on the deck, from May's sobbing over Stuart to Ash's unexpected death, there was only one logical explanation…

"What are you looking at, Shafer?" Rich's words snapped Shafer out of the recollection.

"A… um… I don't know." Slowly, he turned his wrist toward Rich.

"Gobert?" Rich said the word out loud. "I saw that earlier, but I assumed maybe it was from cruise activity. Where did—"

"Klaw," Shafer said the name with all the confidence in the world. "Klaw wrote this on my arm as I was passing out. Right before he left."

Rich squinted his eyes, making his thinking-face.

"I don't understand," Shafer said. "Why would Klaw write this on my arm? What does it mean?"

Suddenly, Rich's eyes snapped wide open and he

jumped from his chair. "Shafer, that's... that's a clue."

"A clue?"

"Yes. Klaw was helping us out."

"Why would he do that?" Shafer pointed to his wrist. "What is this a clue to?"

"I'll tell you everything in just a second. But first, I need to make a couple of calls."

"Wait!" Stuart held up a hand as Rich turned to leave the room. The urgency in his voice seemed to catch Rich off-guard.

"What's wrong, Shafer?"

"I have *one* more question. Something I don't understand... but I gotta know."

"What is it?" Rich leaned against the doorway.

"When Ash attacked me on the deck, I knew he was going to kill me. I could *feel* the life leaving my body, but then... Well, Ash died. Somebody shot him, and that person saved my life."

Very, very slowly, Mr. Brimley nodded.

"Stuart, who shot Ash?"

"Shafer... who do you think?"

*****

Klaw checked his watch. He took a deep breath. He wasn't used to this, this feeling: nervousness. That's what people called it, right? He checked his watch again.

Then he knocked.

The door swung open, and he was greeted by a burly man with lots of muscles—a different one than the first time. He nodded to the man. The man nodded back.

Klaw entered.

Gobert was sitting on the far side of his desk, pouring over a tablet. Eventually, he looked up. He wasn't pleased. Picking up the tablet, he turned the screen around to face Klaw and pointed to a headline that read *Murder Attempted Against Software Tycoon Stuart Brimley.*

Klaw bit his lip. "Funny how fast news travels these days, amiright?"

"How dare you!" Gobert spat the words. "How dare you show your face here after not only failing to deliver the hit, but *also* disobeying my direct orders! Does *this* look like an accident to you?"

Klaw sat down uninvited. "Have you ever had one of those days where nothing goes right?"

Gobert didn't answer. He didn't even blink.

"That's how it was for me," Klaw went on. "I tried *everything,* and I just couldn't catch a break. A car. Poisoning. Even a bomb. And wouldn't you know it—when I finally cave and just shoot Brimley, he's wearing Kevlar. It was a bad day."

"*A bad day?*" Gobert was shouting so loud that Klaw half-expected his papers to go flying off his desk. "This is more than a bad day. This is... this is an utter catastrophe! You're..." He lost his breath, panting for a moment. "You failed to kill him *twice?*"

"Three, technically, if we're counting."

In response, Gobert slammed his fist on his desk so hard that it jarred his computer. "If you're as good as they say, how did you not know that Stuart Brimley was wearing *body armor?* And where the hell did he even get body armor on a damn *cruise ship?*"

Klaw snorted and shook his head. "You wouldn't believe me if I told you."

Gobert was not having any of it. He balled his fists, staring down at Klaw, and fumed, "I should kill you… I should do it right now."

Klaw shook his head, reaching into his jacket and taking out a pistol, which he laid on his lap. "This is uncharted territory for me, too," he confirmed. "But let's not be hasty. Take a deep breath and let's talk, okay?"

Not looking away from the firearm, Gobert let out a long, angry breath. His face was still beet-red, and he hissed out a question. "Do you not realize that the entire FBI is going to be on my ass?"

Klaw shook his head. "Trust me, it's not *your* ass that they're after. It's mine. As you know, all communication between you and I was limited and destroyed. I've shown you. Every bit of digital evidence has been destroyed."

"They'll find *something*," Gobert nearly shouted, but lowered his voice a bit as Klaw put his hand on the pistol once again. "We're talking about the FBI. We're talking about… *Americans*."

"Can't trust them." Klaw picked a piece of lint off his blazer. "*If* they thought you were part of this, they'd take you down. But they don't suspect that, and you'll be fine."

"You can't be certain of that."

"Oh, but I am. And would I lie to you?" Klaw looked at his watch again and tried to level his voice as he prepared to ask his next question. "So, um, let's talk about payment, yes?"

"*Payment?*" Gobert laughed obnoxiously as he said the word. "Seriously… payment? You expect to be paid for a failed hit and a big mess you've created for me?"

Slowly, Klaw nodded. "Yes, actually."

"You're insane. This isn't what we agreed to."

"Then you're a fool if you think I'm playing by the rules."

Gobert squinted his eyes and leaned forward. "What do you mean?"

Klaw sighed. "I'm being reasonable here, but I spent a lot of time, money, and effort planning this, and to be blunt, I know you have the money to throw around."

"Just come out with it! What are you saying?"

Klaw rubbed his chin. "I'm saying that you pay five million dollars for the effort and expense I sank into this mission." He picked up the pistol and waved it for emphasis.

Gobert's eyes locked on the gun.

"Relax, I'm not going to shoot you… at least, probably not." Klaw smirked. "I brought this for self-defense—or in case your guards were armed. You really should consider that, by the way."

Gobert only stared back.

Klaw went on, "But even if I don't plan to kill you, I wouldn't exactly mind accidentally… um, *leaking* your name to somebody at the Bureau."

Gobert's eyes widened. "You wouldn't. That was… that was part of our agreement."

"I'm a hitman! We don't do this by the book." Klaw let out the slightest of laughs.

Gobert, on the other hand, struggled to find the humor in the situation. His face had turned from red to white as a sheet. "You couldn't…"

Klaw took out his phone, holding it up. "You give me five million dollars *immediately* to compensate me for the effort and expenses, and all is well. You don't, and I will call up the FBI this very moment and drop an anonymous tip. I'll tell them you're behind this, and I'll tell them where to find the evidence they need."

Gobert looked like he was staring death in the face."-No... No. I'd turn you in. If they came for me, I'd take you down with me."

Klaw raised his eyebrows. "You'd... turn me in? " He asked the question like he'd misheard. "You'd turn me in with *what* exactly? Do you know where I live? Do you know where I'm from? How to find me? Do you even know *my real name*?"

Realization washed over Gobert's face as he realized he was in an argument he couldn't win. "How do I know you won't screw me over?"

Another shrug. "You don't. You're playing with fire, and that's a quick way to get burned. But if you transfer the money right now, I'll stick to my word: No texts. No letters. No calls. Nothing. Just be glad I'm not asking for more."

After a moment of hesitation, Gobert grimaced and took his phone from his pocket. He dialed a number, made a call, and after having a conversation with the same tone one would talk about death or taxes, he hung up.

"It's done."

Klaw looked at his phone. "Ah, I see. Thanks for your business."

"Leave. Leave *now*."

Klaw stood, holstering his pistol and locking eyes with the bodyguard. Without uttering another word, he exited the office and walked down the stairs, across the ballroom, and saw himself out of the front doors of the empty mansion.

As the sole of his shoes clicked across the walkway, he heard the sirens. They were distant but unmistakable.

Climbing into his car, Klaw began whistling, trying to drown out the sirens behind him. For a while, it worked. Eventually, though, their wail became too strong.

That was his cue.

Klaw put his foot on the gas and rolled forward, away from the sirens, away from the lights, away from the mansion, away from the dozen squad cars stopping outside of it, away from the officers shouting commands and charging the house with weapons, and away from the corrupt man inside.

He left all of it behind, driving toward a better place and brighter future.

A future that, right at the heart of it, had a very special place for a very special teenage boy.

ACKNOWLEDGMENTS:

Thank you all for reading Shafer's second adventure. It was a joy to write and, hopefully, just as much fun to read. That's why I write, afterall.

As always, a few thank you's are in order.

I think God for giving me not only love for writing, but the talent for telling stories and for putting people in my life who help tell them.

Of those people, that includes my mentors: former teachers and professors who have been instrumental in guiding me along the way.

Thanks to my parents, who have really had a heck of a year putting up with me as I started my own business (www.contentninjamarketing.com) and constantly cast my stress their way.

Thanks to the great friends, too. Grant, Mitchell, Tanner x2, and the support group being me.

And, of course, the amazing Skye Norwood. A great friend, yes, but also an editor/writer/coach/cheerleader/gif master who helps bring every one of my stories to life.

Been a bit since I've released a book, but Lord willing there will be more coming down the pipe very SOON.

Big plans, my friends.

More soon,

Jesse

Made in the USA
Monee, IL
22 November 2021